Karen grew up in a small country town in north-eastern Victoria, Australia. She spent her childhood riding horses through beautiful scenery of eucalypts, lakes, and snow-capped mountains and her love of landscape deeply affects her writing. She worked in a range of educational settings and holds a Ph.D and M.Ed (Hons) in the areas of fantasy. She is particularly interested in the power of the hero's inner journey which she explores through Deep Fantasy. Karen has travelled extensively overseas but enjoys nothing more than camping in the Australian Outback. She lives in Melbourne and now writes full-time. You can find out more about Karen and her books on her website.

Connect with K.S. Nikakis

Amazon: https://www.amazon.com/author/ksnikakis
Twitter: https://twitter.com/KSNikakis
Facebook: www.facebook.com/ksnikakis
Goodreads: www.goodreads.com
Website: www.ksnikakis.com
Email: author@ksnikakis.com

WORKS BY K S NIKAKIS

Non Fiction

Journey: Seeking the Sacred, Spirit
and Soul in the Australian Wilderness

Fantasy Novel Series

Angel Caste series:
Angel Blood
Angel Breath
Angel Bone
Angel Bound
Angel Blessed
Angel Caste – Complete 5 Book Series

The Kira Chronicles trilogy (remnant hard copies only):
The Whisper of Leaves
The Song of the Silvercades
The Cry of the Marwing

The Kira Chronicles series:
The Whisper of Leaves
The Silence of Stone
The Secrets of Stars
The Thunder of Hoofs
The Crying of Birds
The Music of Home
The Kira Chronicles – Complete 6 Book Series

Fantasy Novels

The Emerald Serpent
Heart Hunter
The Third Moon
Messenger
I Heard the Wolf Call My Name
Finalist - Best YA Novel Aurealis Awards, 2019

Fantasy Short Stories

The Gift
The Tale of Prince Anura
Dragon Sprite
Glass-Heart
Short-Listed – Best YA Short Story, Aurealis Awards, 2019

THE
EMERALD
SERPENT

K.S. NIKAKIS

First published by SOV Media Australia 2015

Publisher: SOV Media
Melbourne, Australia.

Cover by AS Nikakis: http://asnikakis.com
BeautyStockPhoto/Bigstock

National Library of Australia
Cataloguing-in-Publication entry:
Nikakis, Karen Simpson
The Emerald Serpent
ISBN 978-06482652-3-8

Learn more about KS Nikakis and her deep fantasy books at:

http://www.ksnikakis.com/

For Ms Mandy Kontos – who introduced me to NaNoWriMo, and cracked the whip, ever so gently.

The Emerald Serpent

Thig an nathair as an toll Là donn Brìde,
Ged robh trì troighean dhen t-sneachd
Air leac an làir.

The serpent will come from the hole, on
the brown Day of Bríde, though there
should be three feet of snow on the flat
surface of the ground.
- Gaelic Proverb

1

Etaine moved silently through the mist. Dawn was close, but the land still held by a grey that was neither night nor day. An owl gave voice and a stag stepped from the pines and raised its head. Etaine stopped too and the mist eddied around her like water. *Alainn*, she breathed in the Unremembered tongue, *beautiful*, and then a bird shot from the forest, black wings stark against the mist. Her emerald eyes followed it and when she looked back, the stag had gone. Always the raven, she thought bitterly, as she went on.

Dew soaked her trousers, but she did not pause until she heard the stream, and then she followed its voice ups-lope. The glen narrowed, and the bracken grew thick with lady-fern and then with mosses as she neared the water's edge. Etaine did not know the stream's name but since she had come here with Arturo at winter's start, she had called it Bride after the Goddess. It was fitting for the water gleamed as pure as the Goddess Herself.

Etaine made her way along its bank, her gaze on the pines that clothed the slopes to either side. Their greys were broken by the brilliant white of snow but as the earth warmed, the snow would retreat to the crags; the Fada leave their cots; and Eadar die. Etaine gripped a belt-knife, barely aware of doing so, her attention on the gorge ahead. There, where the walls of the glen drew close and where pine-beauty moths stirred, was the stream's birthing.

Etaine picked her way over the water-smoothed stones into the darkness and pushed the ferns aside to reveal the graven image of a triskele. It had been carved by the Fuaran perhaps, before the ships of Adam's folk had found the Eadar's shores. She set her cakes of chestnuts and dried bilberries on the stone at the Goddess's feet, dipped her fingers into the spring's icy water and brought them to her forehead. Then she bowed, ignoring the pain that erupted in her back. *Bride*; the name was silent in her head, but potent: *I thank you for your healing and wish you peace.*

'The food is for you too, Fuaran, if you will,' she added softly, 'for Bride is generous and shares always.' The cakes were a full day's ration but Etaine was willing to go hungry to honour the Goddess. She cupped the water to her mouth and drank, then rose and pulled her jacket close. The spring's edges were ice-laced, but she lingered. This was the third time she had come here at winter's end to farewell the Goddess, and each time she had wondered if it would be her last. At least if she failed to return, Arturo would know where to bring her signe.

Wintering in the crags was harsh but the real danger

lay in the vales below, as she had found to her cost. But it was not an Eadar Ranger's lot to live as Adam's folk did, with a shingled roof between them and the weather, for the Eadar carried the Goddess's emerald in their eyes and Her ways in their veins, and that made them the enemy of the Fada's gods of stone.

Etaine gave a final bow and made her way back into the pale light of dawn. Music woke behind her like the sound of wind that passes through narrow, stony places or the notes of a flute, but she did not look back. She had heard it here before and in other places where the Goddess dwelt in Her watery forms, and it comforted her as she continued down the glen.

Then, as the first rays of the new sun sparked the mist, she thought of Arturo and broke into a run. He would need help to dismantle the flet if they were to obey Fionn's orders to meet with the rest of the band members at midday.

With Etaine gone, another form of quietness enveloped the spring; one composed of a stag's footfall, an owl's wingbeat, and the tread of a hide-clad foot. The Fuaran crouched as Etaine had and like Etaine, laved her brow with water in honour of the Goddess. Then her gnarled hand slid the cakes beneath her squirrel-skin cape and she gazed in the direction Etaine had gone. The owl turned its yellow eyes that way too, as did the stag, its russet hide a glitter with dew.

'She will not return,' the Fuaran said, her words like the wind's sweet music. 'The Serpent rises. It will end in Lisanisk.' The owl's wings flapped, and the stag tossed its head, nostrils flared but the Fuaran's face remained quiet. 'The wounds run deep,' she said. 'Only time will tell.'

Most of the flet was on the ground by the time Etaine reached where they had wintered, and she stood clear while Arturo dropped the last of the slats through the branches. Her bedroll and pack sat propped against a near-by pine and she gathered up an armful of slats and set off through the trees. Each autumn they must cut new slats of birch and alder, or willow if they were near a large enough stream and construct a winter home high off the ground. And then when winter ended, they must destroy all traces of it.

Etaine zig-zagged through the pines with her burden of slats, pausing now and then to slide them deep beneath the litter. It was a giving back to the earth but mostly it prevented Fada who stumbled on their flet from lying in wait for their return. The southern Rangers made their camps on the ground, no matter the season. They remained band-bound too and had enough Rangers to post guards and fight off attack, but in the north, the harsh winters made forage scarce, and Fionn and Dermot's Rangers wintered in two's and three's.

Arturo had explained the necessity of flets when he had brought Etaine north and while she saw the sense of them, their continuous making and unmaking galled her. They might sleep in the tree-tops, but they still had to vary their fire sites; where they gathered and hunted; and where they trained to improve their chances of surviving another spring and summer in the vales. Etaine would have pre-ferred to winter in caves but most of the larger ones were claimed by bears.

Her life with Lagan in Craith had been luxurious by comparison. Their cot had provided a warm bed each night, a yard well, and a large fire that did not need to be extinguished, but she had walked Craith's streets with her head down and it had been Lagan, not Etaine, who had traded with she- of Adam's blood for everything from nuts and winter roots to cloth to sew a gown.

There had been lesser-Eadar in Craith but few true-Eadar, and none with her white skin, emerald eyes, and black hair. It came from the days Unremembered; the days of the Fuaran and the Serpent. Craith's inhabitants of Adam's blood were tolerant but superstitious and Fada ensured fear of the Eadar's *ungodly* elements was never far away *or* difficult to rouse, as time had proved.

Etaine disposed of the last of the slats, straightened carefully and rubbed the resinous litter from her hands. A throw of scats revealed a *cailleach* hunted nearby and she idly considered a squirrel's drey in a nearby pine. The crags were a hard place to winter for all of the Goddess's creatures and as Etaine made her way back, she wondered how the others of Fionn and Dermot's bands had fared.

This spring marked the fourth that she and Arturo would renew their oaths to serve Fionn for another year and, while the Rangers in Fionn's band had not varied much over that time, she had formed no friendships. Having Arturo had been enough.

Etaine scanned with habitual caution as she walked, noting the bones of a wild cat and a patch of wintergreen, incongruous amidst the snow. She picked a sprig and inhaled its pungent scent. Wintergreen suggested an early spring and she wondered how it would affect Fionn's strategies. Drier ground favoured the horses Fada used to run the Eadar down.

Etaine was almost back to the grove when she heard voices and slid behind a tree. One voice belonged to Arturo, but she did not recognise the second and she drew her belt-knives. The rhythm of speech suggested no threat but she approached in a crouching run, using the pines as cover until she had a clearer view.

The stranger had his back turned which made for an easy kill but he wore the blacks and browns of a Ranger. His hair was brown too which told her he had enough of Adam's blood to rob him of true-Eadar colouring, although even those close to true-Eadar could be brown or red-haired, a quirk that made judging Eadar-blood difficult, especially from a distance when eye-colour was unclear.

'It is well, Etaine,' called Arturo, barely interrupting his speech.

Etaine was not surprised Arturo sensed her presence and the brown-haired Eadar turned. He was from their band and while it took her a moment to recall his name, Donal had no such difficulty with hers. Even if Arturo had not conveniently identified her, Etaine was the only she-Eadar in the northern bands and that, along with her close-cropped hair, made her highly recognisable. And Donal had been at Boath.

'It is good to see you have wintered well, Etaine,' he said, and bowed, the beads in his hair catching the new sun as he touched his fingers to his brow. Etaine bowed too, and kept her face impassive as his eyes drank her in. Her hair was shorter than a Fada's and too short to carry the white, green, and golden beads that honoured the Light, Emerald and Serpent Ways but Donal's interest in her stretched back seven long years.

Donal's blood carried only a small taint, despite his hair colour, but Cormac had cured Etaine of any interest in he-Eadar, especially those close to true.

Arturo explained, in his usual gruff way, that Donal carried a message from Fionn that there had been a change of plans. Instead of meeting Fionn at midday at the Wyche River, the bands were to gather at Mohr Tor by dusk on the morrow instead.

'Mohr Tor?' said Etaine in surprise. 'That is too far west.'

'The Ceannards have decided we are to go to Lisanisk for Bride's Day,' said Donal.

'The Fada gather?'

'They move west too. Whether to celebrate their own foul gods or for some more malign purpose, time will tell.'

Etaine grimaced. Fada were *always* malign but then Arturo spoke again, and Donal's attention swung back to him. 'How many bands gather?' he asked.

'Five go west.'

Etaine started but Arturo was first to respond. 'That is a lot of Rangers,' he said.

Arturo echoed Etaine's thoughts and her unease grew. If Fada wanted a repeat of Craith it would be convenient to have seventy-five Eadar Rangers crowded together in one place. The Ceannards must be very sure the potential trouble warranted the risk *or* be ignorant of the Fada's true nature.

'Whose orders are these?' she demanded.

'Fionn's,' said Donal.

But Fionn's orders would have come from a more senior Ceannard. 'Who is to lead once we are in Lisanisk?' she pursued.

'That is yet to be decided,' said Donal shortly.

The bands Ranged alone and even when they operated as loose affiliates, the Rangers' allegiance was only to the Ceannard whose signe they wore at their necks. But seventy Rangers led by five Ceannards would make command complicated and the Ceannards would probably appoint a Toiseach; a supreme Ceannard all Rangers must swear allegiance to.

Toiseaches were common in the days that followed the arrival of Adam's folk. The Eadar's scattered communities had come together to defend themselves against the invaders but Adam's folk had not wanted to fight; they had wanted only to graze their animals and trade for the Eadar's gem and metalwork. There had been land enough for everyone and so the Rangers had gone back to their usual bands of fifteen to watch over the forests and streams and pass along news of each community's doings as they had always done *until* Fada had arrived. And since then, they had fought for their very existence.

The Ceannards were used to high levels of autonomy and would not want to cede their power, hence Donal's discomfit, but the prospect of a Toiseach held no such difficulties for Etaine. Since Craith, she had fought with a recklessness that numbered her days, and her oaths to Fionn over the years had held more honour than sentiment. As death was inevitable, it made no difference to her who she served.

Sunlight striped the ground with pine-shadows and lit Donal's pale emerald eyes. 'Time hastens,' he said. 'I wish you Fair-Ways to Mohr Tor.' His gaze lingered on Etaine a moment longer and then, with a bow, he disappeared back through the trees.

2

Once Donal was gone, Arturo and Etaine wasted no time in following. Arturo smoothed the litter around the tree that had housed their flet and Etaine fastened her bedroll to her pack and swung it on. The pack was light, not only because she owned little but because she could carry little, and if they must run for any distance, Arturo carried it along with his own.

They set off at a brisk pace and in their usual silence, the lack of speech something that suited Etaine well. Early in their time together, when Arturo's yearning for the forest's quiet places became clear and when Etaine had learned to form sentences again, she had suggested they go their separate ways, but Arturo refused.

'I agreed,' he said, and would not be drawn on the topic again.

Etaine assumed Raghna had asked him to keep her company and if it had not been the crone, then it must have been Blor, for there was no one else. Hand-fasting with Lagan had severed her links with the Rangers and, the lesser-Eadar in Craith who she had counted as familiars if not as friends, were dead.

Donal's visit, with his beads glinting in his long hair,

reminded Etaine she would soon be amongst others and she raked her fingers through her cropped locks as she walked. It had not mattered over winter she owned nothing of beauty, not even beads, for Arturo's hair was unadorned too. She half shook her head. She Ranged only because she could kill more Fada in a band than on her own, not because she craved the company of others, but her thoughts went to the comb Raghna had given her.

It was skilfully carved with the *cailleach*, the owl that frequented Raghna's cave and Blor's cot too, but even it was crude compared to the scrolled silver comb Lagan had gifted her in Craith. Lagan had bedecked her with gemmed necklets and bracelets too, as well as the faceted hair-beads the Eadar had worn since times Unremembered. He had been proud of his true-Eadar wife and, in the end, his pride had cost him everything, including his life.

Chaffinches sang in the pines and their white-barred wings flashed and dimmed as they swooped through sunlight and shadow. They had been common around the cot where Blor had begun her healing and the cave where Raghna had finished it and they were common here too, where Arturo guided her through the trees.

True-Eadar tended towards the solitary but since Craith, Etaine had gone out of her way to avoid others, except for Arturo, who she needed to survive. And even now, when she was strong again, she would have struggled to winter alone in the northern crags. Being with Arturo meant she did not have to spend all her time searching for food, and his massive body provided a warm shell of shelter against the crags' gales and the horror-filled dreams that assailed her at night. But most importantly, Arturo demanded nothing of her, including answers to questions about her past.

Etaine drank from her waterskin as she walked, each icy sip filling her senses with the Goddess's bright presence though not enough to ease her anxiety. She found it difficult to be amongst Rangers, even those she was familiar with such as Fionn's band, and soon she must mix with Dermot's band *and* with three other strange bands as well.

Etaine might curse the hard pickings of the northern pine forests but she loved their solitude, and she and Arturo were safe there, or at least as safe as they were anywhere. And there were compensations. The night skies were filled with the flaming trails of firedrakes made brilliant by the icy air and, when light held the crags, eagles shone as they glided above the snowy peaks.

The fine dawn gave way to a sky filled with patchy cloud and a chill northerly wind and they did not stop to eat until they came to a stand of juniper and birch. Arturo offered Etaine one of his nut and bilberry cakes and when she refused, set it on a nearby stone so that she must take it or let it waste. He knew she had gifted her food to the Goddess, but he said nothing, simply ensured, as he always did, that she ate.

The day drew on and as the wind grew colder, Etaine was glad of Arturo's bulk between her and its gusts. She had not Ranged in these crags and glens before but Arturo went without hesitation as if he followed a hidden path. Despite the cold, the lands were gentler than the northern crags and there were small clearings where blae- and cowberries bloomed in the wintry sunshine. There were patches of early primroses too, pale against the bracken.

The cloud sent an early dusk but the crossbills had gone to their roosts long before Arturo called a halt. They were in a narrow, stony glen and he ordered Etaine to wait and then disappeared up the wooded slope. Etaine paced up and down to stop her muscles cooling. Stiff muscles meant the difference between a fast knife-throw and a slow one; between dying and living to kill again. She checked her belt-knives as she paced, then her sleeve-knives and bent briefly to ensure her boot-knives were in place.

Eadar used short swords and arrows more than knives but she could no longer thrust a sword or draw a bow-string. It did not matter. Blor might have followed the Healer's way but his knife skills were excellent and by the time Etaine had quit his cot, hers were too.

The pines' creak and rattle masked sounds of approach and Etaine strained into the gloom. Before Craith she had avoided Fada she came across in the wilds, but now she stalked them like wolves stalked deer and they knew of her presence only as they choked to death on their blood. Fada ranted that their gods punished the murderous acts of the ungodly but Etaine was more than willing to take her chances beyond the Light Way when Fada inevitably ended her life.

She stilled as she sensed Arturo's return and when he appeared through the trees and beckoned her, followed him up the slope. As the way steepened, pines twisted into odd shapes and the wind's keening grew shrill; its music very different to the mellifluous notes near the spring. A wild cat bounded away, and her belt-knife stayed in her hand as they continued towards a dark gash in the stone. Caves could harbour bears ferocious with hunger after their long winter sleep or even hide Fada, and her steps slowed.

'It is empty,' said Arturo.

Probably because it was little more than an over-hang, but it was dry and out of the wind. There was no sign of others having been there and she slipped off her pack and flexed her shoulders in the way Blor had taught her. Scar did not stretch like skin but Blor's herbal rubs had given her more movement than she had dared hope possible when awareness had first crept back.

She had yearned to return to the emerald vales where

she had wandered in search of death but she had not con-
fessed her wish to Blor; not wanting to insult the Healer
who had fought to reclaim her in his tiny cot, deep in its
grove of sheltering oaks.

The single room she shared with him had been steeped
in the sweet smells of his herbal brews and in silence, for
Blor spoke rarely, and as summer had given way to the
drift of leaves and the deep hush of snow, they had grown
so familiar with each other there had been no need for
words at all. It had cost Blor a year to heal her body and
then he had taken her on a gentle two-day journey, placed
her hand in Raghna's, and walked away.

Arturo did not linger in the cave, just dropped his pack to
the floor and picked up his quiver and bow. 'We will need
a fire,' he said, and disappeared back into the night.

They had eaten little meat in the preceding month and
Etaine wondered why Arturo hunted now. She joked a few
days earlier they risked turning into squirrels on their diet
of acorns, nuts, and blaeberries, but it had not been a complaint. Arturo caught trout, squirrel, and hare in their time
together and it did not matter that lately he seemed content
only to forage. It was certainly simpler, for creatures must
be cooked and their bones, entrails and hides hidden where
other creatures of the wild could find them but not Fada.

Etaine did not need to go far to collect a good supply
of last season's cones. The slope was littered with them,
dried and robbed of their seeds by squirrels and crossbills.
She set the fire as far back in the cave as possible and, despite the cave's entrance being cloaked in shadow and the
wind dispersing the smoke, settled where she could see the
greatest arc of forest. Then she pulled out her sharpstone
and methodically honed her knives.

An owl, wraith-like, battled its way through the

branches' clash, and she wished again the wind would drop. She had not feared the dark before Craith but now she yearned for a distraction from what it might hide. Had the night been clear, she would have searched the skies for firedrakes, but the night was full of storm.

The wind brought the pepper smell of rain first and then cracks of thunder and Arturo emerged from the darkness as the rain began. It sheeted down and, as lightning flashed, the rain formed a gold-lit curtain across the cave's entranceway. Etaine bowed to it, thanking the Goddess for Her bounty and, by the time she turned back, Arturo had set the creature he had hunted on the coals. It looked like a squirrel but it was hard to tell; Arturo had left its head and pelt in the trees for the Goddess's other creatures.

He sat propped against the cave's back and Etaine settled opposite and considered him as she warmed herself. Sometimes the firelight showed him to be more Adam's blood than Eadar, and sometimes more Eadar than Adam's blood, but his height and heaviness were typical of Adam's folk, as was his reddish-brown hair. There were times when Arturo's eyes looked more yellow than green, but he moved with Eadar grace and his speed and sensibility were all Eadar, as was his love of places untouched by a settlement's stone.

He would have fitted easily into Craith but he had also fitted seamlessly into Fionn's band and, as Etaine contemplated him, she was struck afresh by how little she knew of him despite their years together.

Arturo's gaze flicked up and she realised she had drawn his attention. 'It is the right time for you to leave the north behind,' he said.

Etaine's heart quickened and not just because Arturo's words suggested some sort of plan for her. In the last three years, their conversations had rarely gone beyond where to build a flet or the likelihood of finding meat. The north might be harsh, but it was safe and as far as Etaine was concerned, there would *never* be a right time to leave it behind.

3

The storm rolled away during the night to leave the slope's stony hollows a sparkle with miniature springs. They soothed Etaine's disquiet over Arturo's words and she enjoyed her breakfast of cold meat and dried bilberries. Her next meal would not be until nightfall and, as she followed Arturo down the slope, she pondered whether it would be better to live like bears who avoided hunger by sleeping the winter away. You would have to start with a very full belly though, she concluded, and she could not remember a time when she'd had one.

Despite his bulk, Arturo did not need to eat as often as she did and as he provided everything from forage to flets, she had never asked for more. On clear days, when the Goddess's spring was ice-glossed, Etaine could see how sharp her cheek- and hip-bones had grown and when she bathed, the water beaded along her ribs. Thin she might be, but she was strong. She and Arturo barely broke stride as they leapt streams and sprinted up the stone-faced crags and Arturo wrestled her too, giving no quarter for her lightness and scarred back.

She knew he did it to improve her chances of surviving, but it was a long time since she had wanted to live.

16

A squirrel bounded along a branch above her head, the flick of its tail so comical that she smiled. It was easier to keep the blackness at bay when sunlight dappled the forest floor and crossbills hung head down, wrestling cones in their search for seeds. Arturo had said no wild creature ever felt sorry for itself and Etaine suspected it was because they were too busy searching for food or mates. At least she only had to worry about the former, she concluded acidly.

It was mid-afternoon when they came to a fast-flowing stream and Etaine crouched at its edge, delighting in its gleaming stones and the wriggling may fly larvae on its bed. Arturo told her it was called the *Reven* and joined the *Tachdaic River* that passed close to *Ballindalloch*. The next stream was the *Mieg* but it turned east again away from Ballindalloch. The western glens elbowed this way and that, he said, unlike those of their wintering, and so provided places of ambush, deduced Etaine.

'You have been to these lands before?' she asked.

'I have been to many lands.'

Arturo's answer invited no more questions but his descriptions suggested he knew how to reach Mohr Tor before dusk as Fionn had ordered, and so it proved. As the westering sun filled the sky with pinks and purples, steep-sided hills reared from the landscape, their slopes clad in pine, juniper, and hazel, and their summits crowned with stone.

Etaine stared around her as Arturo led her on. They passed a stream and started up a hill that looked identical to the others but, as they climbed, she smelled smoke and glimpsed the glow of campfires. Arturo left her near a small soak and went off in search of Fionn's band, only to appear a short time later to tell her they were the first of their band to arrive.

They set their fire away from the other Rangers' fires and unpacked their bedrolls. The night was milder than those further north and, as the first stars blossomed, toads called from the soak and conversations drifted through the trees. The darker shapes of newly arrived Rangers moved past, some in two's and three's and others in what looked to be full bands. Camps were spaced around the Tor, for there were many good sites, but as the rest of Fionn's Rangers arrived, they settled in a loose circle about Etaine and Arturo.

Greetings were exchanged but conversations did not go much beyond descriptions of their winterings. Fionn was the last of their band to reach the Tor and only nodded to his Rangers before he joined the other Ceannards. The urgency of their discussions took precedence over more formal greetings but that was not the only reason Fionn let his Rangers be. Northern Ceannards understood the harsh northern conditions encouraged independence and Fionn gave his Rangers time to remember the obligations of band membership before asking them to swear service to him for another year. Once taken, an oath could not be undone and any who broke their oaths became outcast.

The chances of survival for solitary Eadar were low, but for Rangers, who were targeted by Fada, they were non-existent. Yet despite their Rangers' oaths, Ceannards were keen to release Rangers who formed mate-pairs to seed children, and the pleasure of Lachlann, Etaine's previous Ceannard, at her hand-fasting to Lagan, had been obvious.

The Bands held high concentrations of true-Eadar blood for Ranging attracted those with the greatest understanding of the times Unremembered and the Ceannards knew, as did lesser-Eadar, that the power of the Unremembered could only survive if true-Eadar children were born.

Etaine wondered sometimes, if that were the root cause of Fada hatred of true-Eadar, but it did not make sense. If Fada murdered those with the greatest potential to Remember the Serpent, they lessened their chances of finding and destroying the creature they hated even more than Eadar; the creature they saw as a rival to their own loathsome gods.

Etaine rolled her shoulders and forced her thoughts back to the Tor. The trees were bright with the twinkle of campfires and she imagined the Tor had looked like this in the mighty Eadar gatherings of old. There would have been music and dance to honour the Goddess, and feasting and coupling as there still were, when Fada brutality allowed it. The Eadar might have danced in the Emerald Way too, and in the Serpent Way, and bowed low to the Serpent to receive Her blessing.

Etaine's sudden sense of the Serpent was fleeting but enough to wake the pain of Ellair's loss. Coupling with Cormac had opened the door to the Emerald and Serpent Ways and while she could still walk the emerald vales, his desertion had slammed the door shut to the Serpent. A hunger stirred that went beyond her empty belly but Donal stepped from the shadows before she could seek the Goddess's comfort at the stream below.

He bowed courteously and settled next to Arturo, but his gaze remained on her and, reluctant to snub a band member so close to formal reunification, Etaine stayed put. Donal carried a mug of mead which he offered her and she thanked him, took a sip, and passed it back despite him gesturing her to keep it. To have mead, Donal must have passed a settlement and Etaine considered their luxuries.

There would be markets with a ready food supply and warm, weather-proof cots like the one she and Lagan had lain abed in each morning while Ellair played on the blankets between them. It had been a comfortable life but an empty one. Lagan's love for her had been intense but she had understood it only because of her love for Ellair. She had wondered since, when all the world had turned to night, whether being robbed of Ellair had been punishment for having robbed Lagan of herself. If it *had* been a punishment, it had been one metred out by the Fada's stone gods, not by the Goddess; *She* held only kindness in *Her* heart.

Donal made small talk with Arturo, but his attention remained on her and she made sure to keep her responses brief. Since joining Fionn's band, she had worked hard at being unsociable; keeping to herself whenever Dermot's band joined theirs and absenting herself from any music and dance. But Donal was not easily put off and she wondered if he had learned an important lesson from Lagan seven years ago in Boath.

Neither Ranger had made a secret of their competition for her as Bride's Day had neared but then Alyn's band had arrived bringing Cormac with it. Donal had stepped back but Lagan had waited his chance, and when it came, had seized it.

Donal had been amongst those who had witnessed her hand-fasting to Lagan and for her to re-appear in the north without her husband, meant she had either abandoned him or he was dead. Either way she was available again. But Donal did not know about Ellair or her oath to never give Fada such absolute power over her again.

The pauses in the conversation grew until Fionn re-appeared and they rose to greet him formally, bowing in turn and clasping the signes at their necks that marked them as sworn Rangers. The signes took the form of a Bride's Cross to honour the Goddess, with creatures at the Cross's centre that identified the Ranger's band. The signes of Fionn's band bore the *cailleach* and it remained the *cailleach* no matter who led them for the choice of creature sprang from the times Unremembered, not from the whims of the Light Way.

Fionn ordered a report from Etaine and Arturo on the state of the crags and surrounding lands, and Etaine was content for Arturo to deliver it. They both had a detailed knowledge of the deer, boar, squirrel, lynx, wild cat, and bear that made the crags their home, and of what their scats told of the other creatures that moved and bred unseen in the higher peaks, but Etaine was struck by Arturo's understanding of what dwelt in the deeper hidden places too. Perhaps it was where he went at night when she woke to find his bedroll empty.

Fionn listened more than he spoke and took more than he shared, which was the nature of Ceannards, but he did confirm five bands had gathered at the Tor: their own and Dermot's from the north; and the southern bands of Gil, Niall, and Cormac.

'Cormac?' blurted Etaine.

'Alyn died in Rosch at autumn's start,' said Fionn sombrely. 'Of fever, not Fada,' he added.

Etaine managed to nod and hoped Fionn interpreted her shock as grief but Donal was not fooled and she had no idea what Arturo knew of Boath. She struggled to attend to the rest of Fionn's words, but it was hard to even breathe with her heart wedged in her throat.

The Ceannards were to meet at dawn, Fionn told them, and if a decision were made to appoint a Toiseach, all the Rangers including the other Ceannards, would swear allegiance to him. The Ceannards' oaths were crucial, realised Etaine numbly, or else they could contradict the Toiseach's commands and the only beneficiaries of the resulting chaos would be Fada.

Given that Alyn had only died at autumn's start, Cormac would be an unlikely choice for Toiseach, she reassured herself. Apart from anything else, he had not had time to build a following, and the risk of him being Toise-ach only arose *if* the Ceannards decided one was needed. Her breathing eased but to survive Fada, Etaine had developed the habit of considering the worst possible outcomes of a situation and she did so now.

While she had no idea how a Toiseach would command seventy-four Rangers, of one thing she was certain: she would never bow to Cormac, let alone swear allegiance to him, and that meant turning north again, probably on her own. The prospect was terrifying, but she hoped it would not come to that. She hoped no Toiseach would be appointed or if one were, it would be Fionn, Dermot, Gil, or Niall. She even hoped that, in a crowd of seventy-four Rangers, Cormac would not notice her presence.

Donal's gaze was piercing but it was impossible to pretend nothing was amiss. Common sense told her that hopes of Cormac being over-looked for Toiseach, and of him over-looking *her* were as fragile as the fire-ash and she felt like snatching back the mead from Donal and downing it in a single gulp. But even as she fought back panic, she realised that none of it might matter. Cormac had been like a sword slash through her heart for seven years, but he had probably forgotten all about her long ago.

A true-Eadar such as him would have enjoyed dozens of couplings by now and his desertion suggested she had left his mind the moment he had left her side. In fact, she probably had nothing more to worry about than her usual concern over how many Fada she could kill before they killed her, and compared to facing Cormac, that was actually a relief.

4

Cormac had chosen the very summit of Mohr Tor to make his camp. He had wanted a clear view of the surrounding lands and the quiet to think, and while he had got his vista, he had not got his peace. The wind's howl through the exposed stone was akin to wolves on hunt. His bedroll lay untouched but at least the stones provided enough shelter for fires to be set and his band to enjoy some warmth. Those not guarding already slept, seemingly free of the worries that beset him, and he continued his prowl between the shards of stone.

Seventy-five Eadar were gathered on the Tor and while there was strength in numbers there was also vulnerability, as Craith had shown. Thoughts of Craith brought the usual boil of anger but Cormac forced himself to calm. Fada were as cold as their stone gods and to defeat them, the Eadar must be equally calculating.

His meeting with the other Ceannards had not gone beyond formal greetings and they had agreed to meet again at dawn to discuss strategies for Lisanisk, including whether to appoint a Toiseach. There had been no violence at the larger Bride's Day festivals since Craith but there were always reports of Eadar disappearances at the smaller ones, and Fada disappeared too, thanks to Rangers.

After Craith, Adam's folk had made it clear they would tolerate no fighting in the settlements they ruled and, as they ruled the larger ones, there had been none, yet thoughts of Lisanisk filled Cormac with dread. While nothing untoward had happened so far, his true-Eadar blood gave him a sensibility beyond the Light Way and he made no attempt to ignore his feelings of foreboding.

A firedrake streaked across the sky and the wind whipped the hair from his face as he followed its trail. His forebears had stood here as he did; watched firedrakes stripe the sky with brilliance; seen the moon grow full and the sun paint the clouds in bright hues at dusk and dawn. They had dwelt in the Light Way as he did, but they had dwelt in the Emerald and Serpent Ways too.

Cormac's breath caught as he sensed the swirl of emerald mists and then they were gone, lost to him like the Serpent Way. It took an effort to unclench his jaw but he was a lot more practiced at shutting out Boath. The damage had been done long before Boath anyway, when his forebears had mixed their blood with Adam's folk and condemned the Ways to the Unremembered.

He continued to pace, knowing he must focus on the perils of the here and now, not on the past. While the other Ceannards felt nothing amiss, Cormac was comforted by their determination to ensure Craith's slaughter was never repeated. Their resolve had been strong enough to bring the bands together and he was certain they would agree to a Toiseach too, for it made sense. And he was determined the Toiseach would be him.

Asgall and Beathan slept with the rest of his Rangers but before dawn they would make their way from camp to camp to learn what they could of the Rangers' mood and, as the bands bathed, breakfasted, *and* exchanged news, would add information to the mix that showed him in the best possible light. Cormac was aware his newness to the band's leadership counted against him, but he had Ranged with the southern bands for many years and his familiarity with them mitigated Niall and Gil's claims as longer established Ceannards.

Cormac knew little of the northern Rangers or their Ceannards, but it did not matter. The Toiseach would be decided by the southern bands because the wants of *forty-five* southern Rangers, who Ranged together all year round, would win out over the wants of *thirty* northern Rangers, who spent much of the year apart.

But selecting a Toiseach was more than just a numbers game or one to satisfy the victor's pride. Disquiet at increasingly lethal Fada attacks had grown even amongst Adam's folk and true-Eadar already knew what it was to fight for their very existence. The Rangers would look for a leader who had the strongest links to the days Unremembered; whose white skin, black hair and emerald eyes best exemplified the essence of what it was to be Eadar, and that gave him a powerful advantage over his fellow *brown-haired, lighter-eyed* Ceannards.

Etaine roused before dawn and sent slivers of ice flying as she flicked back her oiled over-sheet. Arturo's bedroll was empty and she drew her fur-lined hood close as she crouched by the fire and coaxed the coals back to life. The glitter of the last stars was sharpened by the frigid air and, despite the proximity of the other Rangers, the Tor shrouded in silence. The stars brilliance reminded Etaine of the crags and longing surged for their stone and snow and stoic pines; where the demands of survival left no room for thoughts of the past.

But then Donal had walked out of the trees with orders to go west; to join the southern bands; *to join Cormac,* as it turned out.

Etaine's gaze remained on the stars but her head was full of Cormac as she had last seen him. They had circled each other as Bride's Day approached and even in that last moment, she could have stepped back, but his emerald eyes had been as deep as the Goddess's spring. Perhaps she had been dazzled by them and it had been *her* blindness not his that had caused the catastrophic mistake. Cormac's Eadar blood had been potent and while she had known a he-Eadar's heart beat to a different pulse, she had not known it beat to an entirely different purpose.

And yet their joining had been as it should be: on a carpet of oaken leaves beneath the moon's bright silver, and Etaine had been filled with joy and with the understanding that the child a true-coupling promised had been seeded. There had been no need for pledges when two were one as she and Cormac were and the Eadar made anew in a third, and they had exchanged none. But then he had gone, off to Inschbain to rid it of Fada threat. Etaine had been too bewildered to ask why the half band that remained had not included him, but her bewilderment had soon turned to fear.

Cormac had not returned and as the seeded child drew on Etaine's Eadar spirit, an abyss had opened within her that threatened to swallow them both. For three days she had fought to remain whole while Lagan's strong hand had beckoned, offering her his love, his protection, and his *strength*. Lagan's blood was far from true, but it was enough and as the world had darkened around her, she had snatched what he had offered to save herself and Ellair— for a little while.

Etaine was still staring blank-eyed at the sky when Arturo returned, clamped her hands around a mug of boiling water and honey, and guided it to her lips. She gulped down the scalding liquid and, as the Light Way returned, stumbled down slope to where the hawthorn thickets marked the Goddess's watery presence.

The hawthorns tore at her clothes and coated her in iced-beaded webs, but she fought her way through, collapsed onto the frosty bracken at the stream's edge, and laved the freezing water over her face. The cold dulled the pain and she did not rouse until a chaffinch trilled and then, as she numbly considered it, heard voices from the slope above.

Etaine knew Rangers would soon come to bathe and fill their waterskins and she considered which path would avoid them. The Tor's western face was steep and pocked with boulders that she guessed would make it a less popular route, and she hastened off in its direction.

Only pines anchored themselves amongst the boulders, and piles of loose stone made the climb hazardous. She toiled on, the slope so steep in places she used her hands to claw her way up. At least the voices had grown fainter, she consoled herself, their owners having wisely chosen an easier path down. But as she edged her way around yet another tumble of stone, the voices grew loud again, *and* came in her direction.

Etaine swore but before she could move, two Rangers rounded the boulders in front and stopped in mid-speech. Etaine was so relieved neither were Cormac it took her a moment to recognise them: Beathan and Asgall of Alyn's band, Cormac's now, and Cormac's *closest* friends! She wrenched her hood up but they had recognised her too, and shock held them frozen a moment before they bowed and brought their hands to their brows. Etaine reciprocated but more swiftly, so that by the time they straightened, she was past them and hurrying away up the slope.

Of all the Rangers to run into! She swore again as

she clambered over broken tors and, as the slope gentled, strode on with her head down as if deep in thought. She knew it was pointless. Even if Beathan and Asgall had not seen her, with so many Rangers gathered in one place, gossiping with each other, it was only a matter of time before Cormac knew she was there.

At least Arturo had returned, and she joined him at the fire, sitting hard up against him. He must have felt her upset but he simply dragged his pack closer and pulled out more cakes of chestnut and dried bilberry for her. Etaine ate unthinkingly and, to make matters worse, when Donal appeared and offered her strips of smoked deer-meat, she accepted them, and he settled on her other side.

Arturo took responsibility for the small talk once more but after a while the conversation dwindled and Etaine looked up. Donal's attention was on the next campsite where some sort of news was being exchanged and when he rose and made his way over, Arturo followed.

Etaine hugged herself and stared into the fire until heavy footfalls told of Arturo's return. 'There is to be a Toiseach,' he said, and Etaine's heart gave a sickening thud. 'We are to use our signes to choose him.'

'Our signes?' she repeated, aware she sounded like a half-wit.

'Five bands and five bags. We drop our signes into the bag of the Ceannard we favour. The Ceannard with the most signes wins.'

'What …' she began, but Arturo's attention had swung to the Rangers who made their way through the pines. Five of them, Etaine noted numbly, bearing five bags. Arturo pulled his signe over his head and she followed suit.

The Rangers greeted them, set the bags on the ground, and turned their backs. The bags were of coarse weave, emptied of their usual cargo of beechnuts, and roughly marked in charcoal with an owl, a wolf, a lynx, an eagle, and a boar. Depositing her signe in the owl-marked bag favoured Fionn; in the wolf-marked bag, Cormac. The eagle was Dermot's signe, but she had no idea which of the remainder were Niall's and Gil's.

Etaine saw Fionn rarely but she dropped her signe into his bag and was dismayed to see Arturo deposit his in Cormac's. 'Why not Fionn?' she whispered, as the Rangers moved on to the next camp. 'Do you think him a poor Ceannard?'

'A Ceannard's not a Toiseach.'

Etaine stared at him nonplussed. Arturo seemed to suggest Cormac had the best skills to lead *all* the Rangers and by implication, to save the Eadar from the slaughter Lisanisk threatened. But Arturo did not know about Cormac's blindness *or* his desertion; flaws that would risk them all.

'Who do you think will win?' she forced herself to ask.

'A southern Ceannard.'

'You think the southern bands will unite against us?'

'They know each other.'

Etaine wiped her sweaty palms on her trousers. Arturo was right; the contest would be between Cormac, Gil, and Niall. She knew nothing of Gil and Niall, but she hoped with all her heart they were strong, skilled, and admired, because if they were not, she would soon find out whether it was possible to survive on her own.

The summit gave Cormac excellent views of the sunrise but the wind continued to buffet and even the gloriously gilded skies did not ease his tension. At least the meeting went well and the Ceannards had acted quickly, in fact, more quickly than Cormac would have liked. Their decision to appoint a Toiseach and then to immediately begin the process, had given Asgall and Beathan little time to complete their Ranger visits.

But even if Cormac did not become Toiseach, their efforts were not in vain. To fight well, Cormac needed to know the thoughts of the Rangers he fought alongside, particularly those from the north who were strangers to him. He frowned as he considered them. The isolation of the crags attracted Rangers who preferred their own company and who, despite their oaths, were inclined to go their own ways. Whoever became Toiseach must put a stop to that immediately; to defeat Fada, the Eadar *must* fight as a single, unified force.

He tossed more fuel on the fire and settled beside it. He guessed it would be close to midday before the signes were collected and then they must be counted. It was not a task to be rushed. There were many sensitivities involved and the count must be conducted respectfully. The Rangers had been asked to judge the worth of their Ceannards and, while Eadar were known for their shrewd appraisals of character, they were also known for their loyalty.

Asgall and Beathan appeared over the summit's lip and Cormac poured them mugs of mead and listened to their reports. Beathan delivered his in his usual abrupt manner and Asgall more thoughtfully, as was his nature. Despite their differences, Cormac knew his friends told him the truth as they saw it, no matter how uncomfortable or inconvenient.

Beathan confirmed the Rangers of Gil and Niall's bands shared Cormac's sense of foreboding over Lisani-sk, although few could name specific incidents to support their feelings. It followed they would favour a Toiseach who accepted their dread without questioning its source. In other words, a true-Eadar, concluded Cormac.

Information about the northern bands was sparser, as Cormac predicted. According to Asgall, Fionn and Dermot were Ceannards in name more than action and seemed content to let their Rangers operate independently. Cormac's mouth hardened. Whoever became Toiseach would not have a lot of time before Bride's Day to unite even the most amenable of Rangers, let alone those resentful at having their freedoms curtailed, and Fada attacks might begin well before then.

He drained the last of his mead and glanced up to see Beathan exchange glances with Asgall. 'What have you not told me?' he asked sharply. Asgall fidgeted while Beathan avoided his gaze, and Cormac's heart quickened. 'Asgall?'

'Etaine's back.'

Cormac's pause was less than a breath, but something shifted inside him. 'Whose band?'

'Fionn's.'

'With Lagan?'

'No.'

Cormac frowned as if he considered some minor anomaly, but he knew he fooled nobody; Beathan and Asgall had seen him after Boath. 'When did she re-join?' he heard himself ask.

'Bride's Day marks the end of her third year.'

'And she's wintered where?'

'Beyond Carn Goarm.'

Cormac focussed on refilling his mug. 'Not alone, I presume?'

'No,' said Beathan, obviously thinking it safe to enter the conversation. 'With a Ranger called Arturo.'

'I've not heard of him.'

'Apparently they arrived together and have wintered together since.'

'They are a mate-pair?'

They all knew Etaine had hand-fasted to Lagan and that she-Eadar who entered such arrangements insisted on by Adam's folk were inclined to shrug them off later.

'Opinion's split,' said Asgall finally. 'Fionn's Rangers might be called a band, but they know little of each other.'

'Not a useful trait,' said Beathan, 'given what might await in Lisanisk.'

'No,' agreed Cormac, but his thoughts were not on the band's lack of cohesion or even on Fada intentions. They were on a Ranger called Arturo.

5

It was past midday before Fionn ordered his band into formation and led them up through the pines and hazels to the summit. Etaine walked beside Arturo, hood pulled close, head down. Rumours about the likely Toiseach had run between camps all morning and what was truth and what was wild speculation would soon be known. Etaine's clenched hands were thrust deep into her pockets and ravens gave voice as they took to the air, disturbed by the Rangers' ascent. Etaine hoped their cries were not portents or she would soon be making an ignominious descent *alone.*

The Rangers spoke amongst themselves as they walked but Arturo was silent. That was not unusual but the way he sheltered her was. When the stony slope meant she must step right he did too, and when she slowed, he matched his pace to hers. The pale sun cast his shadow over her and she concentrated on staying within it, as if it had the power to protect her from what was to come.

Once they reached the summit, the bands formed a semi-circle around the five Rangers who had collected and counted their signes. The bags at the Rangers' feet were now filled with the signes of their original bands and only the Rangers who had collected and counted the signes, *and* the Toiseach, knew the scale of his win.

The new Toiseach *must* know how many Rangers favoured him, a rival Ceannard, or their own Ceannard, for these things could aid him in his fight against Fada or, if he were ignorant of them, aid Fada.

Fionn quietly addressed his Rangers while they waited. It was the last time they would be in their original band, he told them, for they would soon be members of a new band of seventy-four. As such, they would swear allegiance to the Toiseach and be commanded by him until the next year's Bride's Day.

But Etaine knew if Cormac *were* Toiseach, she would not live to see *this* year's Bride's Day, let alone the next.

A chill wind whistled between the shards and having to wait in it woke the pain in her back. She flexed her shoulders and snatched glances at Dermot, Niall, and Gil. Like Fionn, their faces betrayed neither triumph nor disappointment, but she had no idea what Cormac's showed because she dare not look in his direction.

The Rangers' muttered conversations died away and Etaine braced herself for the announcement, but sweet pipe music filled the air instead. She kept her gaze on the ground, so had no idea who the player was but the notes resonated, and soft swirls of emerald mist eddied about her, carrying with them the Emerald Way's promise of wholeness. She was tempted to give herself up to it, but then the music ended, the mist dissipated, and Cormac was named Toiseach.

An excited hubbub erupted but quieted just as quickly; the Rangers sensitive to the feelings of their temporarily displaced Ceannards. Even so, the popularity of the choice was clear. Etaine had the wild idea of fleeing back down the slope before her refusal to swear allegiance became obvious but the formality of the assembly made slipping away impossible. To make matters worse, the oath-swearing ceremony began immediately.

Gil advanced to where Cormac stood, and his Rangers followed in turn, swearing their oaths as Gil had, and receiving their signes back from Cormac as he accepted their service. A quick scan told Etaine Fionn's band would be last to deliver their oaths, and while there was no way to disguise her departure, at least she had time to thank Arturo for what he had gifted her in their years together.

'I won't swear allegiance to Cormac,' she whispered urgently, 'and that means we part now. I … I thank you for agreeing to be with me. I know I have not been the easiest of company but—'

'No.'

Etaine blinked. It was not a word Arturo had ever used to her before.

'I have given you three years,' he said, 'and you will give me until Bride's Day.'

Etaine's heart pounded. Arturo had never asked anything of her in their time together and nor had he made her feel obligated, but he did now. The oath was a year long, but Arturo demanded far less. And then? Would he accept her desertion? Even join her? Become outcast too?

His gaze was on the ceremony but Etaine was blind to her surroundings, her heart beating so fast she had to suck in air faster and faster to keep up with it. Fionn went forward and then Donal, followed one by one by the rest of their band but still she could not move. And then sunlight bathed her as Arturo stepped from her side.

Those who had taken their oaths waited nearby but the hum of conversation told her their attention had drifted and they waited only for some sort of official ending to the ceremony. Sweat slicked her palms but a grim determination had settled over her and she managed to steady. She had survived Fada and for Arturo's sake, would survive

Cormac, but she would not stay one moment longer than Bride's Day. It was an oath she swore to herself even as she went forward to swear one to Cormac.

His face was harder than she remembered but his eyes were the same: an emerald so dark Adam's folk thought them black. She was aware of the intensity of Asgall and Beathan's regard as they stood to either side, but Cormac looked through her, as she looked through him.

'You take your oath willingly?' he said, asking the ritual question.

'Yes.'

'Then swear it.'

'To the Toiseach I swear my loyalty, my strength, and my service, until this day comes again, or death takes me.'

'I accept your service.'

His voice was as emotionless as hers, but he did not place the signe over her head and for a moment Etaine feared he had seen through the hollowness of her pledge. Then she realised her hood was in the way. She wrenched it back and had a moment to register his shock before the familiar feel of the signe was about her neck again. She managed to bow to the required depth and then her shaking legs took her back down the slope.

The stunned eyes of those who had known her at Boath followed her but Etaine kept her gaze straight ahead until the boulders hid her from view and then she broke into a staggering run and managed to reach the stream before she vomited. Seeing Cormac again had pulled her back into the maelstrom of his desertion and its aftermath of Craith, and all she wanted was somewhere quiet to hide.

She stayed on her hands and knees in the bracken until her belly was empty, then rinsed her mouth in the water, but as she struggled to her feet and turned downstream, Asgall hailed her from above.

'The Toiseach orders his band to the summit,' he said.

Etaine looked to where the water flowed away and patches of avens bloomed as pale as crag's honey, but Asgall's voice sounded again. 'Now!' he ordered, and clenching her teeth, Etaine turned back.

It seemed the *Toiseach* wasted no time in throwing his weight about or getting his underlings to, she concluded, as she clambered up the slope, but when she reached Asgall, he smiled.

'It is good to see you again, Etaine,' he said, as he fell into step beside her.

He sounded like he meant it but Etaine held her tongue, knowing what she said would go straight to Cormac. She braced for an interrogation but Asgall's questions centred on what she had foraged and hunted in the northern crags and she had no objection to sharing what might aid the Rangers.

She spoke haltingly at first, more used to brief exchanges with Arturo than longer conversations, but Asgall's pleasant nature had not changed and after a while she was able to speak more freely. His appearance helped too; his emerald eyes and white skin a true reflection of his blood, despite his lighter hair. Unlike his *friend* Cormac, Asgall might even Remember the Goddess's gift of the two, the one and the three, but she would never know. Her task was to kill Fada, not build friendships.

Cormac prowled about between the shards while Asgall and Beathan rounded up his errant Rangers. His first task as Toiseach was to disabuse them of the notion they could wander off when the mood took them, and the second was to make them aware that any celebration of uniting as a single band was to be earned. At least the delay gave him time to order his thoughts, although thinking of anything other than Etaine was all but impossible.

The fact she had taken the oath astonished him, given her obvious reluctance. He had watched her during the oath-taking ceremony and right up to that last moment had doubted she would step forward, and when she had, it was because of a Ranger called Arturo, not a Ranger called Cormac.

He stamped the frost-hardened ground to expel his anger. The way Etaine shadowed Arturo meant they *had* to be mate-paired and had been for three years, if Asgall and Beathan's reports were true, and before that she had been wife to Lagan.

Cormac's hands came to his hips. Like Lagan, Arturo could not be more than half Eadar, in fact, he looked a lot less, and whatever attracted Etaine, was not his ability to provide for her physical needs either; she was skin and bone.

Cormac stared at the stones sightlessly. If he had not been warned of her presence, he doubted he would have recognised her, so changed was she. He recalled the first time he had seen her. Alyn had brought the band to Boath, deep in the night, but Cormac had been unused to sleeping in a tavern's confines and had quit his room before dawn to take a walk through the nearby oaks. There had been a stream and he had paused to contemplate its quiet flow when she had appeared through the trees ahead, also intent on the water.

Her white skin and fall of black hair told him she was true-Eadar and then she had raised her shining emerald eyes and his world had stopped. She had been shy at first, and uncertain, but there was nothing uncertain about her come Bride's Day. That night she had led him back under the oaks, her eyes luminous and her breasts gilded by the moonlight as she had gazed down at him, her lips parting in a soft smile as she had parted herself to invite him in. And then she had hand-fasted to Lagan and disappeared from his life.

Cormac gripped the triskele in his pocket with such force its points cut his hand. He had traded it in Inschbain to gift her on his return and scarcely knew why he still carried it. Her loss was a physical pain he had hardened himself to, over and over again, and there had been no she-since, whether more Adam's blood than Eadar, or more Eadar than Adam's blood, that healed the wound she had inflicted. And now she was back, the light gone from her eyes as she had sworn an oath to obey him, in a voice bereft of meaning, with a face empty of hope.

Cormac released the triskele and shook his head, as if to dislodge her from his mind. The reasons for the change in her *and* her faithlessness were irrelevant. She was just another member of his band now, one of seventy-four Rangers he was responsible for as Toiseach.

Knowing the bands had placed their trust in him was elating *and* sobering and he reviewed what he knew. Word of Fada movements had made uniting the bands closest to Lisanisk urgent and that had been accomplished. But while Fada intentions were clearly murderous, the intentions of Adam's folk were less obvious, apart from protecting their trade.

It had been trade that had drawn them to Eadar lands in the first place. They had coveted the Eadar's jewelled metalware but had also admired the finely built Eadar with their black begemmed hair, white skin, and emerald eyes, and had wooed and won she-Eadar.

Cormac counted lesser-Eadar amongst his kin and his own blood, like that of other true-Eadar, was not pure. The Eadar had paid a heavy price for these couplings, and for the comforts of taverns and the other strange and wonderful things Adam's folk brought with them.

Cormac's mouth twisted as he considered the part Adam's folk played at Craith. Rumour suggested they were horrified by their unwitting contribution to Craith's slaughter but Craith was five years ago and they had repeated the tale often enough for their part to become more excusable, even honourable. After all, it had been they who had come to the Eadar's aid *eventually*.

It was the nature of Adam's folk to bend in the wind like greenwood, and while he knew they did not mean Eadar harm, their inaction had allowed Fada to harm with impunity, at least until Craith. The violence had so shocked Adam's folk they had expelled Fada from their settlements but the pull of trade was strong and during the years that followed, Fada had inveigled their way back.

And now, as long as Eadar bodies did not litter the streets, Adam's folk seemed content to let the stone gods of Fada multiply in their stone temples and to turn a blind eye to the blood-soaked lands beyond their settlements' bounds.

It did not help the Eadar cause that Fada gods had so little impact on Adam's folk, whose own gods, like those who worshipped them, were willing to live and let live. And yet, despite Adam's folk's magnanimity, Cormac doubted Fada would risk a second and probably permanent expulsion from the settlements, which meant the bloodshed they planned at Lisanisk, would be far less obvious than in Craith.

He took another quick round of the summit as he considered how little he knew of Fada strategies in Craith. It was said the carnage occurred in Craith's main Hall and continued for some time, but he had no idea how Fada confined so many Eadar in one place and blocked all rescue attempts.

Capturing scattered Eadar was easier than attacking a large group, which vindicated his decision to seek the formation of a single *cohesive* fighting force, although he had yet to decide how to deploy his Rangers in Lisanisk. At least the signes revealed he enjoyed strong support amongst the bands and that augured well. Most of the southern Rangers had favoured him *and* over half of Dermot and Fionn's Rangers, although he wagered Etaine's signe was not amongst those in his bag.

Beathan appeared through the stones and Cormac made an effort to relax his expression. 'They are waiting?' he asked.

'Yes, Toiseach,' said Beathan, with a smile.

'Time to begin then,' said Cormac briskly, and strode off through the shards.

6

Asgall parted from Etaine just below the summit but she barely noticed; a dizzying number of Rangers milled about, and she had to fight down panic as she searched for Arturo. But when she found him, he simply handed over her pack and heaved on his own. The Rangers were readying to leave, she noticed dazedly. Cormac and the Ceannards barked orders as they moved through the crowd assigning Rangers to new bands, and the bands and their leaders wasted no time heading off down slope.

Donal disappeared into the trees led by an unfamiliar Ranger and Fionn followed at the head of more unknown Rangers. Fionn nodded to her but did not pause and as the crowd around her and Arturo thinned, Cormac strode over.

Etaine tensed but he simply jerked his thumb towards Arturo, who move forward. Etaine followed but Cormac waved her back. 'Not you,' he said dismissively, and strode off. Arturo held her gaze for a moment longer and then he too was gone.

Etaine gripped her belt-knives to still her shaking hands. The Tor was all but empty and she wondered whether Cormac had abandoned her for a second time.

'No Fada here,' said Asgall behind her, making her

jump. 'You won't need your knives, at least for a while.' Etaine kept her grip on them and said nothing. 'The Toiseach commands we form temporary bands and you are to join mine,' continued Asgall briskly. 'Beathan, you know,' he said, indicating the Ranger next to him, 'and Dugald of course from your previous band.' Etaine nodded and glanced beyond him to where other Rangers waited. 'This is Caitlin and Isbeil formerly of Gil's band,' he said, turning to them, 'and this is Bress of that band too.'

Asgall gave them a moment to eye each other but Etaine was too distracted by Arturo's absence to take much notice of them.

'The Toiseach has set us a little challenge to practise our skills and help us get acquainted,' continued Asgall. 'He orders us to gather at Ballindalloch by dawn.'

'Ballindalloch's a day from here, not half,' said Isbeil.

'The Toiseach wants to test our stamina *and* our ingenuity,' said Asgall.

'Or run us to death,' she retorted.

'Given the distance, we had best be on our way,' said Asgall smoothly, and then his gaze settled on Etaine. 'Where is your bow, *and* quiver and sword?'

The rest of the group looked too. Isbeil's expression suggested she already judged Etaine to be a liability, and Caitlin seemed willing to share her friend's conclusion.

'I use knives,' said Etaine.

'You have to be close for that,' said Isbeil, 'and happy to risk a Fada sword in your guts.' Despite her emerald eyes, Isbeil's olive skin and reddish hair suggested a lot of Adam's blood, as did her willingness to argue.

'The Toiseach might address the matter of weapons later but we have enough amongst us for today's journey,' said Asgall firmly. 'We aren't looking for Fada, just a good strong mead when we reach Ballindalloch's tavern *by dawn*. Let's go.'

Asgall took the lead followed by the two she-Eadar, then Bress, Dugald and Etaine, with Beathan bringing up the rear. They clambered down the slope and when they reached the flatter land near the stream, Asgall broke into a jog and the rest followed.

It suited Etaine to run. The sooner they reached Ball-indalloch, the sooner she would be back with Arturo, but she also knew she could not carry a pack all night.

The she-Eadar spoke together as they ran and after failing to get a response from Etaine, Dugald and Bress spoke with them too. Etaine had not intended to be rude, least of all to her former band-mate Dugald, but Arturo's loss left her disorientated and the band's noise did not help. Even if Beathan guarded their backs, Fada spears could take most of them own before they knew they were under attack. Asgall increased the risk of discovery by calling back warnings of holes or stone-slides, and Etaine longed for Arturo's careful silence.

She fell into her usual rhythm but the burn in her back grew and she considered how much longer she could run and what would happen when she stopped. The she-Eadars had already closed ranks against her and she had never been friends with Dugald or with anyone in Fionn's band for that matter.

As for Asgall and Beathan, their dislike of the she-Eadar who had slighted their friend was obvious, although Asgall made more effort to hide it than Beathan.

The sun dipped behind the pine-clad crags and as darkness thickened, a small moon rose. The band followed the stream's course west, running along its tussocky bank where the going was easier. They were not far from Boath and Etaine knew they would soon pass cots, for Adam's folk penned their animals near water. She and Arturo always avoided cots because they might harbour Fada, and she tried to recall how careful or reckless Asgall was.

The moon gave enough light to see *and* be seen by but Etaine barely noticed. The pain in her back had grown to a roar and she gritted her teeth as Beathan drew alongside.

'Do you know these lands?' he asked as they ran.

'No,' she said, which was not true for she reconnoitred any site she camped.

'You should,' he said. 'We aren't far from Boath.'

'Boath was a long time ago.'

'Seven years ago, come Bride's Day,' said Beathan. 'I wonder what the *she*-Eadar Etaine's been doing in the times since.'

'The same as a he-Eadar,' she said, dragging in air.

'Which is?'

'Trying to stay alive.'

'Oh, *she*-Eadars such as you have more choices than that,' said Beathan. 'They can choose to Range or not to Range; to join with a he-Eadar or not to join; to hand-fast like Adam's folk or not to hand-fast.'

'Or remain alone,' she gritted. Her back was excruciating and dealing with Beathan's badgering made it worse.

'But you aren't alone, are you, Etaine? You couple with Arturo.'

'Not this night.'

Beathan's voice hardened. 'And before that you coupled with Lagan and before that with Cormac. So, is the *she*-Eadar to continue her dalliance with Arturo, go back to Lagan, or choose someone new? Maybe the *she*-Eadar will favour Cormac again, now he is Toiseach. You certainly left an impression on him last time though not a good one, and this time round you might even prove fatal to him *and* to us.'

No he- of Adam's folk had ever spoken so insultingly to her let alone a he-Eadar and she pivoted, drove her elbow into his diaphragm and when he doubled over, wrenched his head back and brought her knife to his throat. Beathan had the sense not to struggle but his chest heaved and then Etaine felt a sword jab between the shoulder blades.

'Release him!' ordered Asgall.

Asgall could kill her with a single thrust but not before she killed Beathan, but Eadar did not murder Eadar, and Etaine let him go, took several paces away and dropped her pack to the ground. Her back was to the rest of the group but she was beyond caring whether Asgall used his sword.

A muttered conversation had broken out behind her, but she did not bother to listen. The Eadar had a long tradition of courtesy between he- and she-Eadar and it was entirely a she-Eadar's decision whether she coupled and with whom. Some she-Eadar never coupled but those who did mostly mate-paired. She- of Adam's blood might go from he- to he- leaving a trail of fractured friendships and feuds behind them, but not she-Eadar, and certainly not Etaine.

She had been eighteen before she had coupled for the first time, *with Cormac*, and it had only been his abandonment of her and Ellair that had forced her to take Lagan. Beathan's fine friend had broken every tenet of the Goddess's creed and yet Beathan had the gall to blame *her*.

'Etaine?' It was Asgall, but she refused to turn, and he was forced to walk around in front to address her. 'Beathan will beg your pardon for the insult, as he must, but now is not the time. We need to keep moving to reach Ballindalloch by dawn.'

'I'm not going with you.'

Asgall's face hardened. 'Is it a *public* apology you are demanding?' Etaine could see how Asgall had jumped to that conclusion but it simply confirmed he shared Beathan's low opinion of her.

'I cannot run any further,' she said, which was half

true. The other half was that she could not run any further *with the pack*.

'We cannot slow our pace,' said Asgall, nonplussed by the turn of events.

'And you won't need to for the *southern* Rangers,' chipped in Isbeil from behind.

'We can rest but then we *must* run again,' said Asgall.

'There is no time for rest,' said Beathan, coming to Asgall's side. 'I thought the northern bands trained through the winter to maintain their strength, but it seems I was mistaken. You will have to run whether you want to or not. Six cannot delay for one.'

'I'm not going with you.'

Beathan's heavy brows lowered. 'You have sworn to!'

'I swore to the Toiseach, not to you.'

'It is the same thing!'

But it was not the same thing, Asgall suddenly saw. Cormac had split them up for his little excursion to Ballindalloch, but he had not formally delegated his authority, in fact, Asgall was not sure whether he or Beathan were in command. The oversight was probably due to Cormac's newness to the role, but it did not help Asgall deal with the recalcitrant she-Eadar in front of him *or* with Beathan's anger, and meanwhile, time slipped away.

'The Toiseach commands *all* his Rangers be in Ballindalloch by dawn,' he said carefully. 'Are you refusing his order?'

'No.'

'Then you need to run,' broke in Beathan.

'Only if we follow the stream. There is a shorter way.'

Beathan had chosen their present route and Asgall felt him bristle. 'There is more than one way to Ballindalloch,' said Asgall quickly. 'The Toiseach made it our destination to see which route each band would choose.' Asgall also knew, as did Beathan, that Cormac wanted to test the strength and obedience of the northern bands as well, and it seemed Etaine had already failed on both counts.

'We are wasting time,' said Etaine, and picked up her pack. 'I will take my own route and meet you in Ballindalloch, by dawn, *as the Toiseach commands*.'

'Wait!' said Asgall. 'I will go with you. I am interested to see whether your way really is quicker.'

'Cormac said nothing about splitting the band,' hissed Beathan, and Asgall drew him aside out of hearing-range of the band.

'I won't be the one to tell him we have lost a Ranger,' he whispered, 'and *Etaine* of all Eadar. She is at risk on her own, especially if she cannot run.'

'Good riddance is all I say.'

Asgall sighed. 'Use your Eadar blood, Beathan, if you won't use your Eadar brains. There is more to this than meets the eye, *more to her*.' Beathan grunted but at least he did not argue.

'The Goddess only knows what Cormac will say about this,' he muttered, and gripped Asgall's arm. 'I wish you Fair-Ways, Asgall, and whatever you do, do not risk your neck for hers.'

Asgall nodded. 'I will see you in Ballindalloch. Fair-Ways to you also, and to those you lead.'

7

Etaine did not waste time wondering what Asgall and Beathan muttered about. She simply seized the opportunity to close her eyes and let herself sink. Before the Eadar had mixed their blood, they had spent as much time in the Emerald Way as in the Light Way and, as a true-Eadar, Etaine had always been aware of its emerald pulse. But it had been distant, like passing a tavern door and seeing the glow of lamps within, *until* she had coupled with Cormac, and then its full glory had been revealed. And the blessings of the Emerald Way had remained open to her, even after Cormac's desertion.

She was aware Asgall had returned to her side and having been gifted the guidance she sought, set off back the way they had come. Asgall's annoyance at retracing his steps was obvious and Etaine sensed his tension rise at leaving the safety of his *friends* behind, but she was happy to be free of their chatter.

She strode along, her pack slung over her shoulder, intent on the map that unfolded in her head. It told her where they must turn, descend, and climb and when she came to the stones the Emerald Way had revealed, she led Asgall away from the stream, through a stand of hawthorns, to the cleft.

Its entrance was filled with years of detritus but she pushed through the leaves and twigs until the cleft broadened into a small gorge. A stream tinkled and star-moths rose as Etaine passed, their wings catching the moonlight that sheened in from above. After a time, the cleft's walls drew closer until the light was extinguished and if it had not been for the moon-fungus jutting from the walls, they would have been in complete darkness.

The gorge continued to narrow until they were forced to shuffle sideways, dragging their packs behind them.

Asgall cursed as he struggled to squeeze through. 'This goes nowhere except the grave and if it gets any narrower, I will have to turn back. I am broader than you.'

'It widens soon and there is a cavern and tunnels, and a climb that exits into a stand of rowans,' said Etaine.

'You have been here before?' Etaine hesitated, reluctant to lie. 'Is that a yes or a no?' badgered Asgall.

'A "no".'

'It is rumoured true-Eadar sense what the ... the Em . . . Emerald Way shows,' Asgall managed to say. 'I will be interested to see if that is correct.'

Asgall's lack of mate-pair made it hard for him to even name the Emerald Way but proving her true-Eadar attributes to anyone, especially Cormac's friend, was the last thing on Etaine's mind. All she wanted was to get back to Arturo. She pushed on as fast as she could and then the walls disappeared, and they were in a small cavern.

'Correct so far,' murmured Asgall.

Part of the roof had collapsed and starlight drifted down to dust the surface of a pool. Etaine had not seen the pool in the Emerald Way but the Goddess did not always reveal Herself. She made her way around its rim in search of its source. She wanted to thank the Goddess but found nothing which meant the water must swirl up from the earth's deepest places, perhaps even from the Serpent's realm itself.

'Have you forgotten the way?' asked Asgall.

'No.'

'We need to keep moving *unless* these tunnels tip us out on the doorstep of Ballindalloch's tavern.' Etaine dipped her fingers in the water and was surprised by how warm it was. 'We need to keep moving,' repeated Asgall.

Etaine turned on him angrily. 'The Goddess must be thanked!'

Asgall muttered something but Etaine ignored him, suddenly aware she carried nothing worthy to gift. Drawing a belt-knife, she nicked a vein in her wrist and Asgall hissed as a stream of red joined the water. Etaine watched the crimson ripples spread. Perhaps if she gifted all her blood to the Goddess she might find Ellair again.

'Enough!' snapped Asgall.

Etaine jolted as if wrenched from a dream and pressed her thumb to the wound while Asgall retrieved a bandage from his pack and bound her wrist. 'That was an overly generous gift,' he grated.

'The Goddess saved me. What would you have me gift Her?'

'Something that won't weaken you further.'

'I am not weakened!'

'You cannot run like a Ranger must and that risks us all.'

'I can run as well as any Ranger!'

'I am sure the Toiseach will be more than happy to test your claim *and* your loyalty. He won't want his band compromised by a damaged Eadar whose allegiances lie elsewhere.'

Etaine's good hand flashed to a belt-knife. 'You think I am in league with Fada?'

Asgall's face hardened. 'Do not play games with me,

Etaine. We all saw how grudgingly you swore your oath and it fits with your behaviour in Boath.'

'Boath?'

'Oh, slipped your mind, has it? Well, it has not slipped the minds of those who count the Toiseach friend. You gave Cormac what he most desired and then took it away again like a child snatches back a toy. It might have been a small thing to you, but I assure you, it was not to him and the last thing the Eadar need is a Toiseach whose focus is anywhere but defeating Fada.'

Asgall's sentiments echoed Beathan's and were probably shared by the rest of the Rangers. She could explain and defend herself but she would have to do so over and over and it would be futile too; the damage to her reputation already as permanent as the scars on her back.

Revealing Cormac had deserted his mate and child would undermine his authority *and* the Rangers' ability to defeat Fada and defeating Fada outweighed any right she had to fairness. Still, the injustice was infuriating, and she could not let the accusation of faithlessness go completely unchallenged, for Ellair's sake, if not for her own.

'When you report *everything* I have *failed* to do to your friend the Toiseach, Asgall, remind him of this: that seven years ago in Boath, it was he who abandoned us, not we who abandoned him!'

She strode off to where the fold of stone hid the tunnel out and while Asgall did not continue the argument, she was so angry that when she reached the tunnel's junction, she could not recall which turning to take. Asgall smiled mockingly but Etaine visualised the pool and then, with shocking suddenness, she was back in the Emerald Way, and she was not alone.

A she-Fuaran contemplated her, then raised her knobbly hand and pointed to Etaine's left. Away in the distance, Etaine saw that Eadar worked a shaft. There were ropes and pulleys and ore glimmered. They metal-mined in the old way, she realised, and the shaft was near the rowans at the tunnel's exit. And then the miners were gone *and* the Fuaran, and she was back in the Light Way with Asgall.

'This way,' she muttered, shaken by the vision. She did not know whether the Fuaran suggested she give up Ranging and return to her metal-working kin in the east or fight to reclaim the Eadar's right to live as they had before Fada intrusion, and she feared her tainted blood robbed her of the insights the Emerald Way had offered.

They reached the rocky slope the Emerald Way had revealed, pulled on her pack and started to climb. The stone provided hand-holds but Etaine's scarred back prevented her reaching for them and she used her legs to push herself up. She was grateful to reach the top and crawl out into the rowans, despite them being bramble-infested. Asgall cursed behind her as he struggled through them but his mood improved when straightened. Dawn was close and there was enough light to see the silhouette of crags and the low rolling plains favoured by Adam's folk for grazing.

'The Drumins,' he said, nodding towards the crags. 'It is not far now. We might even be first to arrive.'

Etaine turned towards the cover of nearby pines but Asgall called her back. 'It is quickest straight west and safe enough,' he said. 'Fada do not come here.'

The southern bands were probably familiar with Fada movements but Etaine's skin pricked as they set off into the open. The land stretched away in a series of rolling dips and ridges that limited vision range to the next crest and they had not gone far when they heard voices.

Etaine jerked to a stop but Asgall continued walking and before she had time to seek cover, four figures appeared on the ridge in front. They fell silent when they saw Etaine and Asgall but kept coming at the same pace and

Etaine hurried after Asgall.

'They are Fada,' she hissed.

'They are Adam's folk,' said Asgall impatiently. 'Fada wear grey.'

The group's low hoods obscured their faces and Etaine's thoughts raced. It would advantage Fada to dress as Adam's folk to take the Eadar unawares and some Fada even looked like Adam's folk, being shorter and stockier, but they gave the tongue of Adam's folk a hard edge *when* they spoke.

Etaine's hands closed over her belt-knives as the group drew inexorably closer and then, with a terrible suddenness, two dropped back and two surged forward in the classic arrow-head of Fada attack.

8

Cormac kept his band at a fast pace but also one that allowed him to observe them as they ran. All were from the southern bands except for Arturo but none from his original band. He had mixed the other bands up as well to break the Rangers' allegiances to their former Ceannards and, to the north or south. To defeat Fada the Rangers must be loyal only to each other and obedient to him.

He had kept Beathan and Asgall together and put them with Etaine and the other two she-Eadar. He had come across less than a dozen she-Eadar Rangers over the years, for although they fought as well or better than he-Eadar, their desire for children meant they left Ranging to couple. Their fighting skills were a loss to the bands, but birthing children was crucial given the Fada's murderous attacks.

Cormac knew it was not easy for she-Eadar to be surrounded by so many he-Eadar, despite the protocols that governed he-Eadar behaviour, and so had placed Etaine with the other she-Eadar. But he was under no illusions simply being she- would seed camaraderie. Caitlin and Isbeil were already close and Etaine's resentment at being under his command was obvious to all. It made it unlikely she would seek friendships with *any* of the *Toiseach's*

Rangers, especially while she had Arturo, and so he had separated her from him too.

Etaine had been highly independent at Boath and even considering she had been cot-bound with Lagan for four years in Allachie, she had spent the last three in the harsh northern crags. Their soaring peaks and frigid vales were difficult to survive in, whatever the southern bands believed, and yet her reaction to being separated from Arturo had been the opposite of self-reliance.

Even as a mate-pair, her need of Arturo surprised Cormac and he watched Arturo as they ran. Arturo went with an easy lope that belied his muscular build and did nothing that made him an obvious outsider. While he did not initiate speech, he responded courteously when others spoke to him, as did the other northern Ranger Raith, and both slowed or quickened their pace according to the band's overall speed.

Cormac doubted Etaine had adjusted to the separation so easily. After they had coupled on Bride's Day in Boath—he cut the thought off. To lead well, he must deal *only* with the here and now. Etaine had left Ranging to hand-fast and live with Lagan and then left Lagan to resume Ranging and mate-pair with Arturo, and now she was under his command and he would deal with her exactly as he dealt with his other Rangers *except* he had placed her with his two most trusted Rangers.

He grimaced. Despite appearances, sentiment had not over-ruled his commander's brain, in fact, quite the reverse. From the moment Etaine had wrenched back her hood to reveal her gaunt face and empty eyes, he had known all was not right with her and, until he discovered whether her malaise risked their mission, she would be watched, either by him or by those closest to him.

As the night drew on, Cormac realised Arturo watched him as much as he watched Arturo. But the lesser-Eadar did not look at him like others of his band did, in admiration or to seek his approval, but in a measuring way. When they stopped briefly to rest and drink, Cormac felt Arturo's eyes on him and when Cormac scanned as he ran, he often surprised Arturo's gaze and, unlike the rest of the band, Arturo did not look away.

While the gloom made it hard to interpret the lesser-Eadar's intent, Cormac sensed no animosity, unlike Etaine. If anything, Arturo seemed curious, as if he found Cormac at odds with some impression he had already formed, and if that *were* the case, Cormac could well imagine where the impression had come from.

Cormac led his band into Ballindalloch as the sun broke the Drumin Crags, the second of the bands to arrive after Fionn's. His Rangers had run well, and Cormac felt tired but content. It was a feeling shared by Fionn's Rangers as they drank mead and ate with Cormac's band before going to their beds. While the tavern was relatively safe, there were cots within the settlement happy to welcome Rangers and there were always Rangers who preferred a roof of branches, especially if those branches were oak.

The sun drifted higher into the cloudless sky and by the time Adam's folk were abroad, carting wood and water, and readying the tavern for the day, all but two of his bands were in. Cormac sprawled at a table in the tavern's front yard as if his only intent was to enjoy the sunshine, but his breakfast of mead, oaten-bread and cheese remained untouched. *All* of the bands should have arrived by now and to make matters worse, Beathan and Asgall's was one of the missing.

Cormac's vantage point gave him a clear view east, the most likely direction of their approach but it was mid-morning before he saw runners in the distance. It turned out to be Niall's band and as they drew closer, the cause of their delay was obvious: Cathal's limp so heavy he was helped along by others.

Cormac hoped Asgall and Beathan's delay was caused by something equally minor but he had learned seven years ago not to rely on hope. His fingers drummed the table and then Arturo appeared with a mug of mead and settled beside him. Cormac was in no mood for company but the lesser-Eadar was so quiet Cormac almost forgot he was there.

The smell of the day's baking filled the air and Cormac strode out beyond the tavern's yard to where he could see to the north and south as well. Asgall and Beathan might have changed their route and be coming from another direction or not be coming at all. Cormac's muscles had stiffened from sitting, and he paced about to loosen them and stave off the fear he had lost the only three Rangers he had ever loved.

He had chosen Ballindalloch because it was relatively safe but nowhere was completely free from Fada threat once Fada had decided their gods should rule the lands. If Asgall and Beathan *had* encountered Fada they might be slowed by injury *or* be feeding hooded-crows.

Something moved behind him and he whirled, his hand on his sword but it was Arturo. The lesser-Eadar moved quietly, despite his bulk. 'Do you search, Toiseach?' he asked.

Cormac found Arturo's phrasing strange and was unsure whether he asked if Cormac *intended* to search for his missing Rangers *now*, or whether the southern bands searched for their missing comrades *at all*.

'We wait,' said Cormac shortly.

Arturo offered no argument and Cormac wondered whether he was as calm as he appeared or simply expert at hiding his feelings. Cormac suspected he would be less composed if it were *his* mate-pair who was missing, as indeed it was. He cursed silently and reminded himself *yet again* his encounter with Etaine had been brief and was long past.

'They come,' said Arturo, so suddenly Cormac started. Arturo gazed east but it was a while before Cormac saw anything at all and relief mixed with surprise at the keenness of Arturo's sight. But his relief evaporated as the band drew closer.

'Seven becomes five,' said Arturo.

Cormac strode out to meet them and clenched his jaw as he took in who was missing. He sent all but Beathan to eat and rest and pulled him aside out of Arturo's hearing. 'Where are Asgall and Etaine?' he demanded.

'Aren't they back? Maybe they have encountered even more wolf packs, bears fresh from their dens, and boar-sows with pups than us.' He smiled humourlessly. 'The only thing we have not had to detour around or climb trees to avoid is Fada.'

Cormac stared at him nonplussed. 'I did not order you and Asgall to break the band.'

'Nor *not* to break it. Nor did you make it clear who had authority or that swearing obedience to you also meant swearing obedience to *us*. And you can thank Etaine for pointing these things out when she refused to run any further.'

'*Refused* to run any further?'

'*Could not* run any further, to be precise.' Beathan paused. 'And I said things I should not have.'

'Such as?'

'About the lovers she has taken and the injuries she caused you in the process.'

'Was this before or after she *could not run any further*?'

'Before. She said she knew a shorter route to Ballindalloch and would meet us here. Asgall went with her.'

Cormac pushed his hand through his hair as he stared back at the direction they had come. 'Do you know which route they took?'

'No, but I can search.'

'Eat and rest. I will wait a while longer.' Beathan moved off after the others and Cormac strode back to Arturo. 'Etaine said she knew of a shorter route here. Which way would she have gone?' Arturo shrugged. 'Would she have lied?' demanded Cormac.

Arturo's yellowy eyes came to his. 'Did your friends threaten her?'

'Of course not,' said Cormac, but he wondered exactly what Beathan had said.

'Then she would not have lied.'

'If she knew a shorter route, why is she not here?'

He had not expected an answer, but Arturo frowned thoughtfully. 'The Goddess might have shown her another route, but it might not have been easy.'

Cormac was far from comforted. He had never known the Goddess to stop an arrow or still a sword slash although in the times Unremembered, the link between the Eadar and the Goddess had been closer. And even now, when the Fuaran were rarely seen and the Eadar shared their lands with Adam's folk and Fada, Eadar sometimes entered the Goddess's realm of the Emerald Way. He had once even glimpsed it himself.

'And presumably the Goddess would have shown Etaine if there were Fada about,' he said sarcastically.

'The Goddess shows what She chooses.'

2

The instant the Fada surged forward, Etaine raced forward too, ducking a spear as she threw her first knife. She aimed for the spearman who shadowed the closest swordsman but there was no time to check the knife throw's accuracy. She leapt sideways as a second spear scythed the air, flung her second knife at the swordsman almost on her and, as it took him in the chest, threw herself under his tumbling corpse, grabbed a boot-knife and hurled it at the second swordsman. It caught him in the shoulder and sent his first slash awry. He charged again and, as Etaine leapt aside, followed, ruining the aim of the spearman behind him.

An arrow sped over her shoulder as the swordsman lunged again and she jumped backwards, feinted, and launched herself under his weapon to his very feet. The Fada long sword meant he must step back to deliver the lethal slash but Etaine's knife sliced across his tendons and, as he tumbled to the ground, she cut his throat.

She pulled his body hard up against her as a shield as she surveyed the scene. The first spearman convulsed on the ground and the second crawled away. Judging by his blood-trail, Asgall's arrow had severed a vein. The two swordsmen were dead. Some distance behind her, Asgall was on his knees, impaled by a Fada spear and she sprinted back.

'Get the cursed thing out,' he gasped.

'Lie down,' she ordered. Asgall obeyed and Etaine cut his jacket and shirt clear. He had been lucky; the spear had taken him in the shoulder not the chest. 'I will push it through,' she said. 'It will do less damage that way.' Asgall did not argue, just grunted in pain as she shoved the shaft further in, snapped the bloodied barb off and pulled the shaft out.

'You have bandages?' she asked.

'You are wearing them.' Etaine pulled her spare shirt from her pack and cut it into strips, then helped Asgall sit while she bound the wound. 'Aren't you going to kill him?' he asked, staring after the crawling Fada.

Etaine tied off the bandage then followed his gaze. 'He is bleeding to death,' she said. 'It will be slow. He will know he is dying and see the world fade; lose everything he loves, piece by piece. Maybe his stone gods will aid him, but I do not think so. I have not seen stone move, have you, Asgall?'

Asgall's face twisted in disgust. 'It is a cruel thing to do.'

'It is the Fada way; did not you know? They bleed children to death. I am just returning the favour.'

Cormac waited at his vantage point some distance from the tavern and Arturo waited with him. The half-Eadar seemed at peace but Cormac paced, his tension so high he wondered whether it would be better for his leadership if he returned to the tavern to rest.

Then Arturo straightened. 'They come,' he said.

Again there was a frustrating delay before Cormac

could see anything and then Asgall and Etaine's approach was so slow he jogged out to meet them. Arturo followed, Cormac having to resist the urge to order him back. As it turned out, he was glad of Arturo's aid. Asgall's shoulder was heavily bandaged and he leaned on a stick.

'Fada?' asked Cormac.

'Yes,' said Asgall. 'I will report in Ballindalloch, if you will, Toiseach.'

Cormac nodded and shifted his attention to Etaine who had taken up position so close to Arturo they touched. Arturo made no show of affection in return which Cormac found odd and, as they started back, Arturo left her side altogether to aid Asgall and Cormac fell into step beside her. 'Beathan's reported your behaviour,' he said curtly, 'and you will explain yourself to me later.'

'Yes, Toiseach,' she said, her gaze straight ahead.

She had a lot of blood on her jacket and his heart quickened as he noticed her wrist was bound. 'You are wounded too?'

'I gifted the Goddess. The rest is Fada.'

Which meant the fight had been up close and very personal. He needed to know exactly what had happened, but he would get Beathan's account first and then Asgall's, not just of the attack but of everything since they had set out. Asgall's cool head would give him a clearer picture of events than Beathan's hot one, then he would compare their reports with Etaine's version.

He had intended the excursion to Ballindalloch to test his Rangers, but it had tested his leadership too and found it wanting. He should have delegated his authority more clearly and yet Etaine had been the only Ranger to exploit his mistake. Had she done so to show him in a poor light, or to hide her inability to run? Or was it just another example of the disloyalty she had shown in Boath when she had refused to wait even a few days for him?

Antagonism, frailty, and faithlessness; qualities that made her a danger to them all *and* to their mission in Lisanisk. Depending on what Beathan and Asgall reported and how Etaine defended herself, he might have to expel her. The idea was shocking and the decision to make a Ranger outcast not one to be taken lightly. Expulsion placed a Ranger in terrible danger, but he would not risk his band *or* the Eadar in Lisanisk for anyone, not even a she-Eadar he had once believed his true-mate.

Expelling a Ranger was far from simple too and she had done nothing this day to warrant it. She had arrived in Ballindalloch as ordered *and* she had probably saved Asgall's life. If he *did* leave her in Ballindalloch, his reasons must be above reproach. The last thing he needed in his band was a debate over whether he acted as a Toiseach should or with all the angst of a spurned lover.

Cormac went to his rooms and bathed, then ate and slept briefly before he visited Beathan, and he was still mulling over Beathan's report when he reached Asgall's rooms. Morgan was just finishing, having cleaned the wound and bound it with a mash to draw out any poisons. He was one of three surgeons Cormac was glad to have in the band and Morgan's news was good. The spear had not done too much damage and the main aids to healing were now food, drink, and rest. Morgan's final comment, that it was not Asgall's sword arm, told Cormac the wound was no impediment to Asgall remaining in the band.

Asgall already looked much improved and Cormac listened to his report without interruption. Asgall did not dwell on Cormac's failure to delegate command but Cormac's oversight was minor compared to Fada disguising themselves as Adam's folk.

'I did not recognise the threat,' admitted Asgall, and

Cormac wondered whether he would have either. At least Etaine's fighting skills had proved equal to the challenge.

'Did Etaine already know the route through the caves?' asked Cormac.

'She said not. I think she used the Em … Emerald Way to find it,' he said, and took a steadying breath.

'Few are able to access it at will,' muttered Cormac, still haunted by its elusive glories.

'Her Eadar blood is strong, as you know,' continued Asgall, and cleared his throat. 'Although I am not sure how reliable the Em … that Way is.'

'Why do you say that?'

'We dropped the Fada corpses down an old metal-mining shaft to hide our presence, but we had to drag them a considerable way back and I was not much help. It was why we were so late. Afterwards Etaine thanked the Goddess for showing her the shaft *the second time*. She said it softly, but I heard.'

'Anything else?'

'It is probably nothing . . .'

'Tell me.'

'Before we left the band, she had been running freely and then suddenly she said she could not run anymore.'

'After Beathan's little lecture on her she-Eadar choices?'

'Oh, he told you about that, did he? Beathan needs to beg her pardon although given her reaction, perhaps she should beg his.' Cormac's eye-brows rose. 'She had a knife at his throat before he knew what had happened and if I had not threatened her with a sword, she might have used it.'

'Ranger against Ranger,' muttered Cormac.

Asgall recalled her accusation of Cormac's abandonment but decided to keep the slur to himself. 'The way she fought Fada …' He half shook his head. 'I do not know if her charge was pure courage or pure recklessness, but it saved our skins. I have never seen anyone fight like that *ever*! She had absolutely no regard for herself *and* she refused to dispatch the last Fada cleanly. She said they bled children to death and that she returned the favour.'

There was a long silence and it was Asgall who broke it. 'I am not telling you how to lead Toiseach …'

'Say it.'

'Something is not right with her and while her true-Eadar abilities and fighting skills could aid us, if she loses control and attacks in Lisanisk like she did today, she could be the death of us all.'

Cormac postponed his planned meeting with Etaine, having decided it was more urgent to discover whether Adam's folk knew of Fada use of disguise. Bress had passed on some disturbing news about Craith too. According to a Ranger from Dermot's former band, it had been unusually dry in the lead up to Bride's Day and Fada had blamed the stagnant springs and sluggish streams on the Eadar's *malevolent* Serpent.

Cormac did not believe the ill-will Fada had seeded had been enough to trigger the slaughter *on its own*, but he ordered his Rangers to report on the state of the springs and streams they had passed. If they were low around Ballindalloch, they might be low further west too.

As he made his rounds of the tavern-rooms, cots, and groves where his Rangers rested or guarded, he passed on word of Fada use of disguise but gave no details of the attack beyond it being repelled. He did not want to add to the gossip Etaine attracted from those who had been at Boath, but nor did he want to highlight her fighting skills given he might expel her.

Adam's folk knew nothing of the Fada's latest strategy and Cormac wondered if it were limited to small groups beyond the settlements. Fada were tall and fair with lean builds and eyes as grey as their clothes and their subterfuge had worked only because of distance. It would be different in Lisanisk's crowded streets. But the ruse could still weaken Eadar trust in Adam's folk and, in further isolating them, made them easier prey.

Etaine set camp with Arturo in an oak grove beside a stream, some distance from the tavern. She was desperate to be away from the band's inquisitive eyes and as she warmed herself by the fire, she grimly concluded the oaks' fragrant darkness was the only good thing she had encountered since leaving the north.

First she had been forced to swear allegiance to the *Toiseach*, an Eadar she had pledged never to see again let alone serve, then the same Eadar had threatened her with interrogation because she had found a better route to Ballindalloch than his *friends*.

No doubt his *friends* had since detailed her every flaw which was probably why he had not bothered to show up, either that or he reinforced how utterly unimportant she was. Etaine shivered and pulled her jacket closer. It was her spare and she wore nothing underneath. Arturo had gone into Ballindalloch's collection of cots to trade for a shirt to replace the one used for bandages and her other clothes lay drying by the fire, having been scrubbed clean of Fada blood.

Two jackets, two shirts, two sets of trousers and underwear; socks and a pair of boots; a comb, a waterskin, two pouches for food; a bedroll and an oiled sheet; flints and a sharpstone; twelve knives and a pack to store it all in. With Lagan she had gowns to wear during the day and gowns to wear at night; soft shoes; silver combs, necklets, and bracelets. She had Ellair too and no signe to bind her to the he-Eadar who had deserted them both.

Etaine tossed more wood on the fire and watched the sparks gush skywards. She yearned to escape the memories by sinking back into the Emerald Way, but the Goddess had been generous this day and Etaine did not want to be greedy. Four Fada were dead and she had escaped to send more into the arms of their stone-hearted gods.

She rose and wandered to the stream where the stars' silver danced on the Goddess's water. It was a cold dance, unlike the flame's golden one, but both held beauty; like the owl-cock and the owl-hen; the fox and the vixen; the he-Eadar and the she-Eadar and, when the time was right, the one: greater than she- and he-Eadar alone, for only the one allowed the third; unless the timing was wrong, unless the coupling went amiss, unless the she-Eadar's judgement was flawed.

Her clenched hands woke the pain in her back and she rolled her shoulders. How she wished Bride's Day was over and she and Arturo far from here! An older wish stirred too: that the Fuaran *had not* retrieved her from Craith; that Blor and Raghna *had not* healed her; that her life *had not* lasted longer than Ellair's.

The wish insulted those who had risked so much for her and it insulted Arturo, who had kept her safe since, and she silently begged their pardons. At least she had this night, she consoled herself, here under the oaks, next to the Goddess's gleaming water.

Arturo did not return until after moonrise and then he brought with him not just a new shirt but the Toiseach's orders that those not guarding were to attend the tavern's celebrations. Etaine cursed but her anger was mitigated by the shirt's softness and ornate metal buttons. It was far finer than her old one and as she donned it, she wondered how much trade it had cost. She had long been uneasy about Arturo spending his wealth on her, but he refused to speak of it, as he refused to speak of who had asked him to be with her three years ago.

'I will join those guarding,' she said, as she slipped on her jacket.

'The Toiseach specifically ordered you to the tavern.'

Etaine swore again as she realised Cormac would use the occasion for his belated interrogation, but Arturo said nothing, intent on setting a trout on the coals. He had obviously fished on his way back but only the Goddess knew how; he had not taken arrows with him.

The flames lit his face as he worked and its familiarity eased her temper. She had often told herself nothing held her in the Light Way except killing Fada, but she would miss Arturo when the Fada killed her. It was the price of letting affection grow but the price of love was many times greater. Ellair and Cormac had taught her that.

The tavern was filled with music, dancing and laughter and Etaine could not wait to leave. There were many Eadar there and Adam's folk, and those whose blood was so evenly split they could call themselves Eadar one day, and Adam's folk the next, and offend no one.

She stopped in the doorway and searched for an empty table, aware of Arturo's unease behind her. Dancers crowded the floor and she recognised Isbeil in the arms of a Ranger she did not know. The she-Eadar wore a dark green gown beaded with gold and topaz and stitched with silver tokens. Etaine had owned similar gowns and her kin still wore them when they celebrated Bride's Day in the east. Isbeil's braid-beads flashed as her partner whirled her about and his clothing flashed too. They must have kin with cots nearby where they stored such finery for it certainly would not fit in a Ranger's pack.

Caitlin was dressed in an equally begemmed gown as she danced with Bress and several unpartnered he-Eadar glanced in Etaine's direction. She ignored them and wove her way through the crowd to a table near the back door. It was furthest from the minstrels and the kitchen, which probably accounted for its lack of popularity but it suited Etaine well. The nearby window not only provided a flow of night air, but an escape route, should Fada join the celebrations.

Once she and Arturo were seated, she examined the room's occupants. Most of the Rangers had replaced their blacks and browns with the bright colours and precious metals of the times Unremembered and Etaine ran her fingers through her short, *unadorned* hair, and smoothed down her shirt. The shirt was no match for Isbeil and Caitlin's gowns, despite its fine buttons, but was better suited to fighting should they be attacked. Anyway, she was only here under orders, she reminded herself, not to find a mate.

A fair-haired she- set mugs of mead on the table, fresh oaten-bread, cheese, and dried bilberries and Etaine nodded her thanks. Cormac must have traded for the fare that celebrated his *acquisition of power* and she recalled that he had never been short of coin. They had been together too short a time to speak of their kin but she guessed that, like hers, they still worked metals and gems into wares for eager and appreciative Adam's folk.

Memories of growing up with her kin now seemed as remote as the Serpent Way. She had left home at fourteen to begin her Ranger training and had moved steadily west, swearing allegiance to a new Ceannard each Bride's Day. She had wanted to see more of the Eadar's lands but she had searched for something else too, and when she first set eyes on Cormac seven years ago in Boath, she thought she had found it.

Etaine tossed back a mouthful of mead but the bolt of sweetness made her head spin and she gripped Arturo's arm to steady. He had not touched his drink and her gaze sharpened on him. The mead might have helped or her time earlier that day in the Emerald Way but for a precious moment she saw into the heart of him, saw him as he was, and then she was back in the music- and laughter-filled room.

Etaine barely noticed, overcome with wonder at the sacrifice he had made for her. 'Go now,' she whispered. 'You have obeyed the Toiseach's command to attend. You need the joy of your own ways and their healing. I am safe here amongst the Rangers.'

Arturo did not look at her or speak; he simply slipped out the door, his outline already blurred as he moved from the light to the darkness. Etaine brought the mug back to her lips, taking care to sip this time as she considered her second attack of blindness. First Cormac and now Arturo; and she had the arrogance to believe she saw with the Emerald Way's acuity!

The music came to an end and the hubbub rose as the dancers sought refreshments, and then the harps and pipes began again accompanied by the soft beat of a drum. The melody was as strong as a river in flood and as gentle as dew. Her mother had danced to it and *her* mother and all the mothers who Etaine counted in her line. The floor filled with she-Eadar and the she- of Adam's folk; with fourteen and fifteen-year old she- just old enough to search for mates; with she- whose children played in the tavern's corners; with crones with star-silver hair and eyes full of knowing. It was Bride's Dance, a dance for mothers or those who intended motherhood, for Bride eased the pain of every labouring she- and looked into every cradle to ensure all was well.

Etaine's knuckles whitened on the mug. The dance honoured the mother past, present and future and not to dance would deny Ellair had existed. She glanced around the room and seeing no sign of Cormac, Asgall or Beathan, made her way onto the floor. The music flowed around and through her and she gave herself up to it, following the intricate steps that brought the dancers together in couples, set them to dance alone and then formed them into threes.

The two, the one and the three of the Light and Emerald and Serpent Ways; of the she- uncoupled, coupled and crone; of the triskele carved in stone or cast in metal to be worn about the she-Eadar's neck in honour of the Goddess.

Etaine was barely aware of dancing for she saw again, as if through a window into another life, Ellair's birth and when the pain had stopped, how the crone had placed him squirming on her belly. She felt again the suck of his baby mouth on her breast; the delicious smell of his skin and later as he grew, the sound of him as he laughed and looked up at her with Cormac's eyes, filled with Cormac's love.

10

Cormac stood in the tavern's doorway and watched Etaine dance. Her face had been expressionless since she had come south but now it shone and even from across the room he saw the joy in her emerald eyes. No doubt her thoughts were on the child she planned with Arturo or on the child *she already carried*. The revelation was like a sword slash, but he forced himself to confront it because it explained why she had suddenly refused to run last night, fought the Fada so fiercely, and let the Fada bleed to death.

They bleed *children* to death, she had told Asgall, and so she had done the same to them. She-Eadar were renowned for the ferocity with which they defended their young and her carrying fitted with her cleaving to Arturo, for she-Eadar stayed close to the fathers of their children early in their seeding.

Cormac's jaw tightened as the complications multiplied. Until a she-Eadar's belly grew, she could fight as well as any he-Eadar and he knew of she-Eadar who had Ranged until a few months before they had birthed, but not when full-blown battle loomed. Her carrying did not give him the reason he needed to expel her *yet*, but he was determined it would; for her sake, her mate's sake, and for his band's. All he had to do was create the right set of circumstances and he would be free of her forever.

The dance ended and Etaine settled back at her table and took a sip of mead. It was the first time she had managed to dwell on Ellair's life rather than his death and she wanted to hold onto the moment for as long as possible. She ignored Isbeil's speculative gaze and the stares of other Rangers but under the onslaught of their curiosity and the minstrels' new tune, the precious sense of Ellair began to slip away.

Desperate not to lose it, she shut her eyes and felt herself sink but before she reached the blessed emerald vales where he still might dwell, a chair grated, and she was jerked back to the Light Way. Cormac lounged at the table beside her, his gaze on the dancers. He was dressed as plainly as she was in the blacks and browns of a Ranger, but clear, gold, and emerald beads glinted in the depths of his long black hair.

'So, you tired of your comfortable cot with Lagan,' he said, 'or did Allachie prove too small for the Etaine who had roamed the crags? Or did you sicken of being the *obedient* wife? Worse than having to obey a Toiseach, was it?'

His tone was mocking but like him, Etaine kept her eyes on the dancers. A casual observer might have thought they exchanged pleasantries about the evening, unless they knew them.

'It was Craith,' she said.

'What?'

'Lagan took me to Craith.'

'But his kin are at Allachie.'

'Yes.'

With their fine houses and fine clothing and fine suspicion of all things Eadar. Lagan's father had cast his lesser-Eadar mother adrift, but he had not seeded another child and it was better to have a part-Eadar son than no son at all. But taking Etaine to Allachie with her emerald eyes and her Eadar powers trailing after her like a demon shroud had been a step too far. Even hand-fasting had not helped.

Cormac was silent, no doubt thinking of the news that had seeped like a blood-red tide over the lands five years ago; of how Adam's folk had been used by Fada; of the rumours Fada had seeded of evil abroad; of the encirclement, burning and murdering that had followed. A terrified mob could be extremely efficient killers, as Fada had proved.

'Lagan's dead?' he asked.

'I have to hand it to you, Toiseach; you have lost none of your wits.'

'So you re-joined the Rangers.'

'Eventually.'

'Why did you leave?'

Cormac's change of tone was so sudden her eyes jerked to his. He still lounged in his chair but there was nothing relaxed about him and then his dark emerald eyes came to hers, filled with pain. 'Seven years ago, Etaine. Why did you leave?'

'Why did *you*?'

'I did not leave,' he said, clearly puzzled.

'Inschbain. Do you not remember?'

'There was Fada-trouble there,' he said, still obviously confused. 'I went with the half-band.'

'Who cleared Fada out in two days,' she said, which she knew for a fact because messengers had gone back and forth and despite her agony, she had managed to hold on. But Cormac had not returned. 'You abandoned us.'

Cormac's brows had drawn, and she saw how he struggled to make sense of her words. 'It was Bride's Day festivities; you know that. I stayed a couple of extra days, that is all. Your band was with you in Boath and half of Alyn's band. There was no abandonment.' And then as understanding dawned, his expression changed to incredulity. 'You left with Lagan because I did not rush back to your side? You left out of spite?'

'To spite a blind man would be a low act indeed,' she gritted. 'Lagan offered me what I had most need of. Once you had gone, I had no choice.'

'This is childish, Etaine. I was only gone for—'

'You abandoned us!'

Images of Ellair as she had last seen him swamped her and she struggled to her feet. Cormac still looked at her but now his face held bemused contempt and his dishonouring of her and Ellair was unbearable. She retched, managed to get to the door, and fled into the night.

Cormac sipped the mead and even ate the bread and cheese Etaine had left untouched, but he tasted nothing. For seven long years he had let her desertion eat away at him like a canker, only to discover her motivations were as petty as a sparrow's squabble over snails. He had completely misjudged her character. He had thought her many things over the years but never mean-spirited.

He gulped down the remainder of the mead and picked up the second mug, Arturo's probably; Etaine's chosen mate after Lagan's death. But he set it down again untasted. No Eadar could afford to be drunk and even those who danced, did so with knives in their boots. He supposed he should feel sorry for Etaine for losing Lagan, but he did not.

Etaine's beauty and true-Eadar blood made her everything a he-Eadar desired and she would have no trouble acquiring a third mate if she tired of Arturo, or a fourth or fifth. And yet in the scheme of things, none of it mattered:

not her faithlessness to him, or Lagan's death, or what unfolded with Arturo. What mattered was what he must do as Toiseach to keep his band safe.

His fingers drummed the table as he considered his options. The simplest thing would be to set a trial his Rangers must complete but she would fail. That way it would be clear he was bound to exclude her from the band for her own safety. Ballindalloch lay in the shadow of the Drumin Crags and a run up one of their peaks would present his Rangers with very specific challenges, especially if he mixed the bands in a particular way.

By refusing to run in Asgall's band, Etaine had shown her unwillingness to risk the child she carried, *if* she carried one, so there would be no danger of her pushing herself beyond her limits. The trial, and its outcome, would be obvious to all.

The decision to expel Etaine did not bring Cormac the relief he craved, instead he felt resentful at being forced into such a position. At least his band enjoyed themselves this night, even Asgall on the dance floor now, somehow managing to embrace a sandy-haired half-Eadar, despite his arm in a sling. Etaine had saved Asgall's life but Cormac reminded himself he was responsible for the welfare of *all* his Rangers, *and* the Eadar who would gather in Lisanisk to celebrate Bride's Day.

The dance came to an end and the dancers swirled about the tables in search of new partners. The pretty redhead whose gaze he had felt more than once swept into a mock curtsey in front of him, the low dip ensuring a good view of her breasts nestled in her lacy bodice.

'A dance, Toiseach?' she asked, eye-brows raised in a way suggestive of more than a brief encounter on the oiled boards.

She was more Adam's blood than Eadar, but Cormac was in the mood for things other than grim musings on

Etaine. He smiled and rose, his hand skimming the smooth skin of her back as he took her in his arms. She pressed against him and as his blood rose, he doubted they would see out the dance. The floor was already less crowded and even as he gazed about he saw couples slip away. There was a passageway to one side that led to small rooms and he manoeuvred her towards one, but she tugged away.

'Outside,' she whispered, but Cormac shook his head.

He had not coupled under oaks for seven years and he would not now. The redhead pouted but her annoyance was short-lived. The bed in the room he chose had a straw mattress that was hard but clean and she was quickly distracted. Cormac was a skilled lover and took care that no she- who welcomed him ever regretted her choice, but he slipped away as soon as he could afterwards and out into the cool night air.

He could hear the stream's voice and see the darker crowns of the oaks that sheltered it. Seven years ago, Etaine had opened a place in him nothing had filled since and now she lay under the oaks again, with Arturo this time, and likely carrying Arturo's child. For a moment his chest heaved as if he had run and then he turned on his heel and strode away into the darkness.

11

The sun had yet to rise when Etaine picked her way along the thick growth of bracken at the stream's edge. Arturo followed, for the first time choosing to accompany her on her early morning swim. He had a calmness about him too she guessed came from being given permission to be as he was, and she was glad.

They passed falls of glittering wood-moss, primroses, and beech-fern but recollections of her exchange with Cormac robbed her of her usual enjoyment of them. The *Toiseach* had not appeared at their camp afterwards, despite his earlier threat to question her, so either he was satisfied with his *friends'* version of yesterday's events or had decided not to waste his time on a *spiteful child*. He might be right, she sneeringly conceded. Choosing him seven years ago *had* been childish.

They came to a stand of rowans where the stream elbowed out into a quiet pool, undressed, and slid into the water. Arturo had deep scratches down his back but Etaine said nothing about them just as Arturo had never spoken of the scars that gouged hers. The water was silvered with mist but anger over Cormac continued to rob her of pleasure and after a while she pointed to the shore. Arturo nodded but continued his gentle swim and she picked her way up the bank and wiped and shook the wetness from her body. Then, as she bent to retrieve her shirt, she looked straight into the moss-green eyes of a she-Fuaran.

Etaine knew it was a *she* even though the Fuaran's craggy face might have belonged to a he- as might her squirrel-skin cape. Etaine bowed deeply and when she straightened, the Fuaran had gone. Then something pale caught her eye amongst the bracken. It was a posy of primroses, she saw, tied with a reed. It could only have been left by the Fuaran, and given its nearness to the pool, as an offering to the Goddess.

Etaine wondered if she and Arturo's swim had interrupted the Fuaran's worship, but that was not all that troubled her; there had been recognition in the Fuaran's eyes. Perhaps the Fuaran had been one of her rescuers at Craith and had come to see how she fared but that suggested Etaine was special, and she had sensed other Eadar there that terrible night, in the hidden waterways, under Craith.

It had been so dark she had imagined herself dead, had wished it; had thought the stream that carried her along and the sparkling caves and tree-roots that passed overhead had been part of the Serpent Way. But there had been Fuaran with her in the water, their silver hair floating about them as their gnarled hands kept her face to the air and the Goddess's water to her back, quenching and cleansing her wounds. The blessedness of oblivion had taken her, until weeks later, awareness had drifted back in Blor's cot.

Arturo sloshed from the water carrying a wriggling trout, but she said nothing of the Fuaran and held her silence while he dressed and they made their back to camp. Donal waited there but his smile faded as Arturo appeared from the oaks behind her.

'The Toiseach orders his Rangers to breakfast well and meet in the tavern's yard before the sun breaks the crags,' he said. 'We are to explore their heights today and travel light. That means weapons but no packs.'

'Another pointless excursion,' muttered Etaine, after Donal had gone.

'To climb well, the Rangers must trust each other,' said Arturo, as he gutted the trout. 'And to fight well, the Rangers must trust each other too.' Etaine continued to scowl as Arturo put the trout on the coals and raked out the sweet chestnuts he had roasted overnight. 'Today will be a long day,' he said. 'Eat.'

Etaine ate.

Most of the Rangers were in the tavern's yard when Etaine and Arturo arrived and they were far more subdued than on the previous night. Etaine guessed some had imbibed too much mead or had slept too little, or both. The tavern was quiet as well; its shutters closed against the early morning chill; its fires reduced to slender streams of chimney smoke.

Cormac was not quiet though or dull-headed. He strode about flicking his fingers and barking orders as he assigned his Rangers to this or that band, and the yard soon emptied as the bands set off towards their designated peaks. Etaine stared at the Drumins' ragged outline while she waited. They were smaller than the northern crags but steeper, with only occasional stands of stunted pines to break the grey of their stony slopes.

Etaine hoped Cormac would leave Arturo with her but Beathan soon summonsed him, pausing briefly to beg her pardon for his *disrespect* of the previous day, before he headed off. With Beathan's band gone, only she, Asgall, Cormac and two sandy-haired Rangers remained. Cormac disappeared back into the tavern and Asgall took the opportunity to introduce the sandy-haired Rangers as Artair and Tormod who, despite their physical similarity, were not related.

They had been raised in the surrounding lands, Asgall told her, and were familiar with the Drumin Crags *and* with Cairn Toul, the peak they were to climb. The sandy-haired Rangers nodded to her but made no effort at conversation, just paced about in a way that reminded Etaine of Fada horses. They had the same nervous energy and their rangy builds suggested speed.

'I'm to stay here,' said Asgall, patting his sling, 'but I will make sure there is roasted meat and plenty of mead to welcome you back.'

'We will need it,' said Cormac, striding back. 'We have a day of climbing ahead. My Rangers must be as fast on the crags as they are on the flat and those who aren't are a danger to the band. The tavern-keeper tells me the wind will turn by noon and that means rain. It can make Cairn Toul perilous, but we have the speed and strength to reach the peak and be on our return journey well before then.'

His hard gaze fixed on Etaine. 'We travel light and will need our hands free to climb so no packs, swords, quivers or bows. That will suit you, Etaine and, unlike your journey here, allow you to demonstrate your full speed and strength. Let's go.'

Etaine was used to running in the northern crags with Arturo but the pace Cormac set was unrelenting. He took the lead and Artair and Tormod followed, and none of them glanced behind to see how she fared. Artair and Tormod shared a fierce rivalry Cormac fed by keeping just ahead of them, and while neither challenged for the lead, they fought to show themselves in the best possible light. They talked as they ran and laughed occasionally with Cormac, and while his exclusion of her was glaringly obvious, the younger Rangers need to beat each other made them oblivious to all else.

Etaine's anger grew as she ran. She did not care they drew ahead but it meant she missed their brief rest breaks because as soon as she came level, Cormac led them off again. His little speech before they left and his behaviour since, made it clear he sought an excuse to expel her, and nothing would have suited her better than to be quit of his odious company. But she had pledged Arturo to remain until Bride's Day and that was one pledge she was not going to break.

Cormac's behaviour reinforced how poor her judgement had been seven years ago in Boath, but Etaine was no longer that naïve eighteen-year-old with a child to protect and she searched for quicker routes to the peak as she ran. Cormac had chosen a path that snaked between slabs of sheer-sided stone but as they climbed higher, the stone to her right disappeared to reveal a dizzying drop. There were no signs of other paths or of the pines she had seen from below and then, just as the tavern-keeper had predicted, the wind swung, and clouds built. The tavern-keeper certainly knew his weather, conceded Etaine, but his timing was out. They were still a long way from the peak and even if they sprinted, which the path did not allow, the rain would beat them.

Etaine had no idea whether Cormac had reached the same conclusion and sought shelter with his *friends*, because she had lost sight of them. Like the northern crags, Cairn Toul was fractured in places but most of the clefts she passed were little more than lairs for lynx or cats. In the north, there had been larger caverns, some joined by tunnels and even by shafts that provided a way to scale the crags from the inside.

The shafts she had explored with Arturo were dark and slick with bat droppings, but Etaine pledged that if she found a shaft here, no matter how perilous, she would risk the climb. The opportunity to beat Cormac to the peak was too good to miss.

The wind grew chill and as the clouds darkened, she stopped at a cleft. It did not smell of any creature and she slid inside. It was shallow but a circle of fire ash told her others had been there. It was a relief to be out of the wind and she was tempted to stay put, but her *disobedience* would give Cormac the excuse he needed to expel her, and she turned back to the entrance and stopped.

There was something on the wall and her heart leapt. Carvings of a triskele! They ran in a continuous line around the cleft and given their height above the floor, she guessed they had been carved by Fuaran. Etaine traced them with her fingers as she made her way slowly around the cleft and emerald light twined about her like a bramble's new shoots.

The triple spiral of the uncoupled, coupled and crone; the two, the one and the three; the Light and Emerald and Serpent Ways. She murmured thanks to the Goddess as she went and had no idea how much time had elapsed before she arrived back at the cleft's opening and stepped outside.

The return to the Light Way was violent. A blast of icy wind rocked her back on her heels and lightning cracked. Etaine hastened on along the path but the wind and sheer drop to her right made the going hazardous. Empty sky loomed ahead as the path swept around the peak's exposed shoulder and, as she considered how best to navigate it, a squalling gust all but sent her over the edge.

Thunder boomed and as rain deluged down, she searched for finger holds on the sheer stone to her left.

'Etaine!'

She looked up, blinking savagely to clear her eyes. Cormac crouched on the ledge above and she glimpsed the dark smudge of a cavern behind him. No doubt his *friends* were already snug inside. He was dangerously close to the edge, leaning out, his hand stretched.

'Etaine! Quickly!'

Etaine let go of the stone and stepped back. Cormac offered her nothing more than abandonment, as this day had proved again. She half thought of turning back to the triskele-carved cleft but before she could move, a torrent burst free from some impediment above, gushed down the stone and gouged the path from beneath her feet. She pitched forward and there was a sickening jar as her chest hit the path's edge, and then she was falling.

Cormac stared at the empty space in horror then staggered into the cavern and sagged against the wall. 'Etaine's fallen,' he said hoarsely. They were well short of the peak, but it did not matter; the fall would kill her. Well, he had wanted her out of his band and out of his life, and he had got his wish. The understanding was terrible enough but her rejection of the aid that might have saved her, was like a sword blade through his heart.

'She might not have fallen far,' said Tormod. 'Cairn Toul has a reputation for being unquiet; for its clefts to open and close in rains such as these. Some believe Fuaran still haunt these crags and have the Goddess's blessing to send Her waters this way and that; others say the stone is easily dislodged to reveal and conceal clefts in turn. We can search for her once the storm passes. It should not last long.'

Tormod sat with Artair at the back of the cavern speaking together softly but Cormac remained at the cavern's entrance, staring out into the rain. Rangers could suffer fatal accidents like anyone else but the brutal truth was Etaine's death was anything but accidental and if he had kept them together, they would have all been safe in the cavern. The bitter realisation came to him that having her in his band had been the first real test of his leadership and that he had failed it catastrophically.

Beathan and Asgall had not wanted him distracted by old wounds being torn open but if he had been the Toiseach the Rangers deserved, Etaine's return should not have mattered. He led seventy-four Rangers, and none were identical in their temperaments or skills, or in what they had endured before he had taken command.

And Etaine had survived Craith! The only Ranger he knew of who had! Yet he had ignored the chance to question her; to learn from the battle they had lost, how they might win the next one.

The rain continued to pound and while Cormac had no idea of the truth of Tormod's claims of shifting clefts, the young Ranger was wrong about the storm's duration. It lasted well into the afternoon.

He waited until the rain was a light drizzle, then led what remained of his band back to where Etaine had fallen. The path had gone and they had to pick their way around a gaping hole.

Far below he could see the dark crowns of pines where Etaine had probably landed, but Tormod's fanciful claim she had only fallen a small way gave Cormac the excuse he needed.

He would send Tormod and Artair to search the clefts and slopes immediately below, while he went straight to the pines. He needed to reach her body first and when he did, he did not want witnesses.

12

There was darkness and cold but Etaine's awareness ebbed and flowed. Clouds drifted overhead or were they water-shadows under Craith? Panic threatened she must endure the nightmare again; hear Ellair scream for her; smell herself burn. Gnarled hands passed her along as they had before and dank stone was so close to her face she imagined she was in a tomb. A belief Fada *had* killed her in Craith and she had been laid to rest in a rocky grave, rattled about in her brain and then fell silent like everything else.

The next time awareness crept back it was to the sweet smell of burning cones and the delicious warmth of flame. Stone was gritty under her cheek but she did not move for movement required strength and she had none. She managed to screw her eyes around but everything was smudged, even her hand resting motionless on the stone, and she used her ears instead.

The muffled sound of rain brought back memories of falling and then a soft brush of hair touched her face as someone leaned over her. Disembodied hands pressed something warm and wet over her cheek, its pungent reek reminiscent of the poultices Blor used, and she drifted again until a bony hand shook her awake.

The poultice was gone and she could see enough to make out a she-Fuaran crouched on the stone in front. Seeing her awake, the Fuaran rose and beckoned and Etaine lifted her head, vaguely surprised she could do so, then used her hands against the stone to lever herself into a sitting position. Every bone in her body felt bruised but nothing felt broken. The Fuaran beckoned again and Etaine concentrated on getting to her knees and then to her feet.

The cavern swung around her like water in a bucket and the Fuaran waited until Etaine had steadied before she moved off and Etaine forced her shaking legs after her. The Fuaran did not look back but she went slowly, leading Etaine through tunnel after tunnel. Etaine had to bend double to navigate some while others soared, full of glittering pillars. A chill, rain-drenched draught heralded an opening and Etaine followed the Fuaran through, stopped and blinked in the brightness.

The storm had left a clear rain-washed sky but the light told her she had lost most of the day. She was still a long way up the mountain and only a little above one of the pine groves she had seen from the tavern's yard. The pines would have given them shelter from the storm, but Cormac had deliberately chosen an exposed route. Antagonism flared and the Fuaran's head swivelled as if she felt it too.

The Fuaran continued down a pebbly path to where pine needles clothed the stone and Etaine calmed as she breathed in the pines' resinous scent. The light was muted under the trees and the silence disturbed only by the wind's soft sigh through the needles. She followed the Fuaran on to the grove's edge, to where the slope gave way to a precipitous drop, and when the Fuaran stopped, Etaine stopped too, careful to keep a respectful distance.

The Fuaran glanced back at Etaine then pointed to her

left and Etaine looked that way but saw nothing unusual. 'There is nothing …' she began, turning back, but the Fuaran had gone.

Etaine stared about her nonplussed. She had no idea what she was supposed to see but the Fuaran had taken a lot of trouble to bring her here and the least she could do was search for whatever it was. She went on through the trees to the very edge of the grove but the only thing out of the ordinary was a blackened pine.

The lightning strike had not been recent and the charred trunk was clad in new growth. She idly brushed the soft green needles, surprised to see her fingers dusted in golden pollen. Despite the pine's catastrophic wound, it had repaired itself and even given birth to new life.

Etaine's breath caught and she collapsed onto a nearby log as understanding swept over her. 'Sweet Goddess,' she groaned, and cradled her head in her hands. The Fuaran's message was plain but the path it marked out for her was so much harder than killing and waiting to be killed. It required hope and trust, and the risk of being betrayed all over again, and Etaine doubted she had the strength to turn along it.

A footstep sounded and her head jerked up. It was Cormac and for once he moved unwarily, his gaze flicking between the tree-tops and the needle-covered ground. He searched the trees' crowns for branches broken by a falling Ranger and the ground for the Ranger's broken body, hers to be precise, and he was almost to her before he sensed her presence.

In an instant he was crouched, knives drawn, and then his face betrayed such a bolt of emotion it was as if no time had elapsed between now and Bride's Day in Boath. Etaine trembled as, in the Emerald Way, two halves of a golden arc sparked into being, its shimmering bow close to completion.

'How is it you live?' he whispered, his face as open as it had been that night under the oaks.

Etaine had no answer and he came to her and ran his fingers gently down her cheek. His eyes were full of the emerald light that could knit two Eadar and make them one but even as she surrendered to it, the light extinguished. 'That's a nasty bruise,' he said, using his hand now to appraise the injury. 'Can you see out of that eye?'

'Yes, Toiseach.'

'Just as well. A half-blind Ranger's a danger to the band. Wait here while I summon Tormod and Artair. They search further afield.'

Etaine watched him disappear back through the pines and her newly woken hope wavered. Cormac had abandoned her and condemned their child to death and yet she sensed something had shifted, not in Cormac, but in herself. She had long known hatred exacted a price and that there were still beautiful things in the world she had closed herself off from. It was as if Fada *had* killed her in Craith, not because they had murdered the most precious thing in the world to her, but because they had murdered her willingness to love.

The understanding came to Etaine that while her body had survived the star-brand, her spirit had not, and yet the part of her able to give and receive affection was not beyond healing, as the blasted pine had shown. A want for love had woken, sudden and unlooked for, and while what she had shared with Cormac was dead and gone, there was potential for more than the emptiness she had endured since Craith. She did not want a mate and nor would she seed another child, but the need to have a he-Eadar's sweet mouth on hers while their bodies joined was suddenly overwhelming.

Cormac re-appeared with Tormod and Artair and they set off down the path, Tormod again speaking of the curious nature of Cairn Toul's clefts. Etaine did not bother to listen; how she had survived the fall and the part the clefts or Fuaran had played, swamped by the surge of her blood. All she thought of were the he-Eadars in Cormac's band who could give her what she wanted and how quickly.

The she-Fuaran emerged from the pines and settled on the log Etaine had vacated, and then an owl glided to the ground. The stag remained on the gentler lands away from the peak's sliding stone, but he watched there, and he listened.

'She was blind to the flowers at the pool but she sees now,' said the Fuaran. 'And in the he-Eadar, the Emerald Realm wakens.'

'Yet even there he refuses her!' The owl's talons gouged the needles and the Fuaran waited for her to settle.

'He refuses himself,' said the Fuaran gently.

'He risks her!'

'She risks herself,' the Fuaran countered. 'But the risk is less now. He will follow.'

'He has *never* followed!'

'The link grows stronger; soon it will complete. Then he will know as she does; see as she does.'

'We have *no* time!' exclaimed the owl and speared away through the trees.

The Fuaran remained where she was, her moss-green eyes on the blackened pine. 'She sees now,' the Fuaran repeated softly, 'and soon he must too.'

13

Etaine found coming down Cairn Toul a lot easier than going up, despite her residual dizziness. Rain had slicked the path but Cormac kept the pace gentle, apparently no longer intent on proving her worthlessness! Not that she cared; she was too busy sifting through possible partners for the night. The Ranger needed to be of the southern bands so that after Bride's Day, she would not see him again, and he needed to be content with only a passing moment of pleasure.

She dismissed Tormod and Artair, despite them being from the southern bands. She craved the potency of a true-Eadar and that meant a Ranger with the white skin, black hair, and deep emerald eyes of the times Unremembered. Donal's Eadar blood was strong despite his lighter hair but he was of the northern bands and being older and more determined, would be difficult to shrug off.

Who else? It did not help she had never taken any interest in the other Rangers, but Asgall remained at the tavern to organise a communal meal and that meant mead and mixing well into the night. With over seventy Rangers to choose from, it would be easy to find one willing to share himself with her.

Cormac called a rest break when they came to a second grove of pines. A waterfall slid down the slope like a silver ribbon, pooled briefly in a stony basin, then flowed away. They drank and replenished their waterskins, and then Artair and Tormod settled on a nearby log. Etaine remained beside the pool, scooping the cool water over her bruised face.

The Goddess's voice sang in the water's chime but Etaine's enjoyment was ruined by Cormac's prowl behind her and she closed her eyes to shut him out. In an instant she was in the wondrous landscape of the Emerald Way, where emerald drifts hinted that the joy of Ellair's presence might still be possible. But then Cormac's voice intruded, calling her name, and she reeled in confusion thinking that somehow, he was there with her.

'Etaine?'

The Emerald Way dissipated and she was back in the Light Way with Cormac crouched beside her, his dark eyes filled with the emerald light he had wrenched her from.

'Where is it you go?' he whispered.

'Somewhere better than here with you,' she muttered, disorientated by the violence of her return. She had never gone into the Emerald Way so quickly before, nor so deeply, and she struggled to make sense of her surroundings.

All softness left Cormac's face and he stood. 'Time to leave,' he said.

Cormac ordered Tormod and Artair into the lead and fell into step beside Etaine, holding his silence until his temper cooled. He had resolved to treat Etaine exactly the same as his other Rangers but it was hard when she insulted him to his face! And her ability to enter the Emerald Way at will and refusal to speak of it, added to his anger. As Toiseach he needed to consider *anything* that might aid them against

Fada and that included the other Ways, no matter how remote they seemed.

The mystery of how she had survived the fall from Cairn Toul added to his frustration.

He dismissed Tormod's claim she had fallen into a cleft; to avoid being horribly injured, she would have had to conveniently landed in a pool as well. Her clothes *were* wet but that did not prove anything; thanks to the deluge, his were wet too.

She kept her gaze straight ahead and his lips thinned as he brought his steps into rhythm with hers. 'Do you remember falling?' he asked.

'Yes, Toiseach.'

'And landing?'

'No, Toiseach.'

'You could not have landed in the pines from where you fell,' he said. 'In fact, you could not have survived the fall. Did you stay conscious?'

'No, Toiseach.'

'Do you remember *anything*?'

'I woke in a cavern. A Fuaran took me to the pines.'

'A Fuaran?' Fuaran were reclusive and he had only glimpsed two in his entire life. 'Why would a Fuaran do that?'

'To show me a lightning-blasted pine that had regrown.'

Etaine looked at him as she said it, the intensity of her gaze reminding him of how she looked at him in the pine grove and Cormac's skin pricked. He had missed something and the understanding added to his aggravation.

'Rest when we get back,' he said shortly.

Her face swivelled again, angry this time. 'Why? Because you think me weaker than the rest of your Rangers? Because you want to expel me?'

'Because unlike you, the rest of my Rangers have not

fallen off a peak!'

'You do not know *what* has happened to the rest of your Rangers this day, Toiseach!'

Her answer was true but infuriating. 'My main concern is not the effects of your fall but whether you carry,' he said, keeping his voice low. 'You joined the she- in the Bride's Dance last night and I have seen you retch more than once. *And* we are in the season when Bride smiles on Eadar seedings.'

'Oh, and I suppose that like your *friend* Beathan, you think the father could be any Eadar *or* Adam's folk I have taken a passing fancy to.'

'As Toiseach I need to know the vulnerabilities of my band! I won't take Rangers into Lisanisk who cannot scale walls, run, or fight hand to hand. One band member's failure could mean the death of many. I am asking you directly, Etaine: do you carry?'

'You are blind, Cormac,' she said bitterly. 'How is it with your true-Eadar blood and your true-Eadar eyes, that you are so blind?'

'Answer me!'

'Do you think *any* she-Eadar who had been at Craith would *ever* risk seeding a child?'

Her eyes blazed but as she strode off she hugged herself as if in pain. Cormac cursed under his breath, reminded again of his failure to question her over Craith. And he could add his total inability to remain detached to his list of shortcomings! Well, he would rectify every one of his failings before the night was out, and he would begin with a dispassionate analysis of her behaviour.

She had positioned herself exactly midway between him and the two other Rangers as if she made a point of spurning everyone's company, but in truth, true-Eadar tended towards the solitary. It was what attracted them to Ranging, that and a fierce need to protect other true-Eadar who were the target of Fada attacks. But given the attraction between true-Eadar, why had Etaine chosen a mate who carried so much blood of Adam's folk?

Maybe her choice of Arturo was a reaction to Lagan's death, as if she sought protection in a mate who was taller and more muscular than a he-Eadar. Her feelings for Lagan must have run deep, given she agreed to the Adam's folk custom of hand-fasting, and yet she had chosen *him* as a mate just a few days earlier.

Maybe she had coupled with Lagan *before* Alyn brought Cormac to Boath and he had simply been a dalliance. The idea was repugnant, but it was not the only reason Cormac dismissed it. Experience told him he had been Etaine's first coupling and his glimpse of the Emerald Way confirmed their coupling was true.

So why had she hand-fasted with Lagan and left? Because in not hastening back from Inschbain, he had *abandoned* her and the band members who remained in Boath! Cormac ground his teeth in vexation. The charge made no more sense now than it did when she had hurled it at him in the tavern. And that was not the only mystery that plagued him. Etaine had danced the Bride's Dance and now she not only denied carrying but insisted that, after Craith, she would *never* carry. And that meant she had just lied to him.

His ire rose but he reminded himself of his resolve to remain dispassionate and forced himself to search for other explanations. The Bride's Dance celebrated motherhood, so if she did not carry now, and had no intention of carrying in the future, the only explanation was that she had carried in the past.

Cormac stumbled to a stop as her words to Asgall after the Fada attack, and the reason for her gauntness and aggression, became appallingly clear. Asgall had warned him of her volatility earlier but Asgall did not know the full depths of Etaine's suffering: that she had birthed a child with Lagan and lost it to Fada.

Cormac lengthened his stride to catch up with his band but he struggled to shake off his feelings of horror. He must still question Etaine about Craith but it made the task even grimmer and knowing the cause of her violent and erratic behaviour did nothing to lessen the risk it posed when they reached Lisanisk.

14

Even with the storm's delay, Cormac's band was the first to reach Ballindalloch, which was not surprising given they had turned back well before the peak. He ordered Etaine to her camp to rest and then he and Asgall made a quick inspection of the tavern's yard where they were to eat. The meal would be the last they would share as a band of seventy-five, for even if they all survived Lisanisk, they would revert to smaller bands afterwards to ensure sufficient meat and forage as they Ranged.

A boar roasted over the fire and its delicious vapours filled the air, but any possibility of a happy evening was marred by the prospect of dragging Etaine back through Craith's bloody events. Yet he had no choice. For his Rangers to defeat Fada in Lisanisk, he must know *exactly* how Fada had defeated Rangers in Craith.

Asgall had achieved a lot in the band's absence but there was still much to do. Fresh kills of hares had to be skinned and gutted, and there was bread to be baked and eggs to boil. He set Artair and Tormod to replenish the fire fuel, haul water and set the mead barrels in place, while he started on the hares, positioning himself next to the main fire to receive each band's report as they came in.

As the day wore on and his Rangers returned, he learned the storm seemed to have focussed its attentions on Cairn Toul and there had been no other injuries. His Rangers had seen nothing unusual either, nor sighted Fada, which did not mean Fada were absent, given Etaine and Asgall's encounter yesterday. Nor did it mean Fada were unaware of *them*.

The Ceannards had discussed the dangers of bringing so many Rangers together but had decided the risk to Lisanisk's Eadar warranted it. They would be breaking into smaller bands tomorrow in any case and taking different routes to reconnoitre the lands around Lisanisk. The trek would not be demanding but it would be dangerous. They could not avoid the larger settlements where Fada congregated, and Fada horses gave their riders reach and speed.

Cormac tossed the jointed hare into the pot, washed his hands in a bucket, and made his way to the tavern's kitchen in search of salt. He was annoyed to see Etaine there, despite his orders to rest. She made bread with the tavern's servers and he paused in the doorway to watch her work. One side of her face was bruised the colour of her eyes but she seemed well enough. She had rolled up her sleeves and wore an apron to keep the flour off her Ranger's garb as she kneaded and flipped the dough. This was how she had lived with Lagan in Craith: making meals and eating with him *and* their child each evening.

There was a whole part of her life she had excluded him from and resentment flared, deep in his guts. If she had not spited him by taking Lagan, it would have been he who had shared her life these past seven years; he who had lived with her in peace as his kin still did in the east; he who had fathered her child.

Children played around the table and he watched her offer a knob of dough to a little he- of Adam's folk whose chin barely reached the table's floury edge. It was a simple, tender gesture and Cormac's resentment grew as she smiled as the he- took it. And then, as if she sensed Cormac's presence, she looked up.

At her oath-taking she had looked straight through him and since then she had avoided eye-contact or glared at him in anger or contempt, until today. For the first time in the pines on Cairn Toul and again as they trekked back, her deep emerald eyes had actually looked at him, and she looked at him now; not with the sort of questioning of earlier, but with disappointment, as if she had weighed him up and found him wanting.

The Rangers assembled around the fires to eat and as the sky darkened, great swirls of stars blazed until the heavens were more silver than black. The Rangers' good humour increased as the night went on but so did Cormac's dread. Etaine had smiled in the tavern's kitchen and he was surprised how much he wanted that smile to stay.

He moved from group to group sharing mead and laughter over comical mishaps his Rangers had suffered during the last few days. He learned that Etaine had blamed her bruised face on a slip during the storm, which was true as far as it went. He guessed she refrained from criticising his behaviour to keep his leadership strong, and he supposed he should be grateful that she hated him marginally less than Fada.

But even as the thought crossed his mind, he realised he had never sensed hatred from her, just anger and pain. But why? Cormac shrugged off the nagging unanswered question. Like the rest of his Rangers, Etaine was entitled to her private thoughts and feelings, as long as they remained private. But one thing that was not private was her coupling with Arturo. Out of seventy-five Rangers, she was the only one mate-paired, although there could be others, he conceded, who were more discrete.

If Etaine had told Arturo the truth about her fall, Cormac might have to deal with an angry lesser-Eadar before the night was out *or not*. Cormac's breath sifted between his teeth. Etaine's choice of mate was yet another puzzle but the attraction was certainly strong.

She had sworn allegiance to Cormac only to avoid being separated from Arturo and she had barely left her mate's side until Cormac had forced the issue, and yet tonight, she was not with Arturo at all.

Cormac frowned. They had not stayed in the oaks long before returning to the tavern, although long enough to couple, he supposed, which might be why Etaine felt content enough to mix with others. But mixing with others was out of character and as she wandered from group to group, she looked anything but content.

Cormac's attention on her sharpened and while he continued to mingle with his band, he chose a route that kept her in sight. She stopped at a group of younger Rangers at one of the smaller fires and he saw them straighten, and then she half turned so her back was partly to two and her attention clearly on the third. Cormac stiffened; he scarcely believed what he saw. It was a quintessential courting gesture used by both he- and she-Eadar and the other two Rangers moved away.

Cormac scanned rapidly. He could see no sign of Arturo but Asgall had noticed and his face was heavy with disapproval. Cormac had cautioned his friends against publicly criticising Etaine for choosing Lagan seven years before, but what she did now was different.

She- of Adam's blood caused discord by moving from he- to he- and the last thing Cormac needed was that sort of conflict in his band. Gossip ensured Rangers knew of Etaine's hand-fasting to Lagan, and her pairing with Arturo was obvious, but he suspected few Rangers knew of Lagan's death.

If Arturo went after the Ranger Etaine had chosen, the band might divide along southern and northern lines, or between those supportive of she-Eadar rights and those who believed in she-Eadar responsibilities. He needed a unified band to defeat Fada; not one that wasted its strength in brawling.

Cormac swerved so his route took him between Etaine and the young Ranger, and the denser oaks where they headed. The Ranger had been a member of Niall's band and for a moment Cormac struggled to name him. *Taig*; that was it. He was fast and a strong fighter but it was his true-Eadar colouring that made him stand out; Etaine had made an obvious choice of partner for the night.

They were already some distance from the fires and Cormac quickened his pace and then faltered as he became aware of Arturo in the shadows. The lesser-Eadar's gaze followed Etaine's progress but his emotionless face took Cormac by surprise. To lead well, Cormac needed to understand his Rangers, but when it came to Etaine and Arturo, he understood nothing at all.

He cursed and broke into a jog to increase the arc of his approach and then dropped back to walk as he came back through the oaks. Taig saw him first for Etaine's attention was on the young Ranger by her side and the softness of her expression riled Cormac even further. Taig bowed in formal greeting but Etaine said nothing, and even under the oaks' dense canopy, he caught the angry flash of her eyes.

'I regret interrupting your stroll,' he said to Taig, 'but I have urgent matters to discuss with Etaine *and* Arturo, and as we leave tomorrow, they must be discussed now.'

'Of course, Toiseach,' said Taig, and with another bow, moved off back towards the gathering.

Cormac waited until he was out of earshot before he turned back and by then Etaine's fury was plain. 'You have no right to interfere,' she hissed.

'The band does not need the distraction of a she-Eadar hand-fasted to one Ranger, mate-paired to a second, and coupling with a third!'

'Lagan's dead!'

'Even if the band knew that, you coupling with Arturo *and* Taig at the same time can only cause strife.'

'You are blind Cormac! You look but you refuse to see!'

He took a step closer. 'We are discussing *your* judgement, Etaine, not mine and for a true-Eadar, it is *extraordinarily* poor.'

'Yes, so poor I even coupled with you once!' She laughed contemptuously. 'Oh, how young and stupid I was, Cormac, but unlike you, I have learned! And I have seen! You have learned nothing and you see nothing!'

Her repeated accusations of his blindness infuriated him. 'This is not about Boath, Etaine, it is about Lisanisk! And it is about Craith and what Craith can teach us. You know things most Eadar did not live to share and I *need* to know what they are. You will give me a full report *this* night at the tavern. *Now*!'

He stormed off, summoning Arturo and Beathan as he went and then Asgall. The privacy of the tavern was the best place for the interview where there would be no interruptions or witnesses. The tavern-keeper had shown him a suitable room earlier and Cormac snatched up a jug of mead and some mugs from the kitchen and went there.

15

Asgall lit a lamp and Cormac snapped the shutters closed, excluding the starlight and the happy sounds of his band. There was no fire in the grate, but the room was not chill; it was simply cheerless. The only furniture was a scrubbed wooden table and bench seats and he waved Arturo and Etaine to them. Asgall and Beathan sat opposite and Beathan poured the mead, but Cormac remained standing. He had not had time to share his intentions with Asgall and Beathan, but they knew him well enough to hold their tongues.

He wanted his friends there to catch anything he missed, and he wanted Arturo there for Etaine's sake. She must relive Craith's horrors and would need comfort afterwards and given the insults she had just hurled at him, the *Toiseach* was not the one to offer it. She still glowered at him, but her knuckles had whitened on the table's edge and she sat close to Arturo.

'As we know, five years ago come Bride's Day, Fada carried out a murderous attack in Craith,' he began, 'and we think they plan another, this time in Lisanisk. Before Craith we did not believe their hostility went beyond hateful rantings and occasional violence but no Eadar believes that now, whether Ranger or other, and since Craith, it has been a matter of kill or be killed. We have learned the hard way what Fada are capable of, but we now have the advantage of a survivor of Craith who can tell us exactly what Fada did that day.'

Asgall and Beathan's surprise was plain and their gazes flicked between Arturo and Etaine.

'Etaine?' prompted Cormac.

Etaine looked physically ill and Cormac's guts tightened. He had assumed that while Lagan and their child had been killed, Etaine had escaped capture, but now he was not so sure. Arturo's face told him nothing but Etaine's distress was clear. The silence stretched but he had to know what had happened that day or risk it repeating.

'We need to know Etaine,' he said.

The bruising was stark against her ashen skin and her voice trembled when she spoke.

'Fada tainted the springs around Craith leading up to Bride's Day. It sickened the children of Adam's folk and killed their animals. Fada set fires and burned some of their own temples, sure signs, they said, of the Serpent's fiery breath. The Serpent had roused, they said, drawn by the evil of the gathered Eadar, and because the Eadar drew the Serpent with their foul blood, the Serpent would break free from its underground tomb where Fada gods had banished it.'

She took a shuddering breath. 'Fada said that true-Eadar had the power to turn the Serpent back but had refused. True-Eadar wanted the Serpent to enslave Adam's folk because Adam's folk had helped Fada enslave *it*.

'Not everyone believed their vile preachings but there were enough . . . especially when the children fell ill and the contagion of fear spread. On Bride's Day, mobs led by Fada rounded up true-Eadar and held us in the Hall; those who resisted were killed, as were Adam's folk who tried to protect us.'

She looked at Cormac for the first time. 'Lagan died because he refused to abandon us.' Cormac said nothing and after a long pause she continued.

'Once we were in the Hall, Fada locked out Adam's folk and barred Craith's gates to the Rangers beyond the wall. Fada believe the doors to the Emerald Way open on Bride's Day. Five years ago, they decided the doors were in Craith. All they needed was a true-Eadar to tell them exactly where and how to gain access. Then they could enter and destroy the Serpent.'

'They would not have found an Eadar able to do that,' said Asgall slowly.

Everyone in the room knew there were no words in the Light Way to describe the Serpent's abode, let alone how to reach it. Silence stretched, broken only by Etaine's harsh breathing and the attention of those gathered came back to her.

'They used the star-brand,' she began, and faltered. 'And when that did not work . . . they … strung up … the children … and … bled them … to death … in front of … their parents.'

She had pressed so close to Arturo there was no space between them, and while his face remained curiously expressionless, Asgall and Beathan's showed shock at her words and dislike for Cormac for having wrung them from her. Cormac could not blame them; he wanted the horror to end as well.

'And did the Fada learn anything?' he forced himself to ask.

'No.'

Arturo still made no move to comfort Etaine and Cormac found his behaviour incomprehensible. If *he* were her mate, he would be at her tormentor's throat by now.

'And how did you escape?' he pursued.

'The Goddess sent storms . . . that quenched Craith's fires and what . . . fed the fear of Adam's folk. She sent bolts and . . . one struck the Hall. Fada claimed it was proof the Serpent wreaked its destruction . . . but that was a mistake. Bride's springs had long provided for Adam's folk, and those who had weapons used them against Fada. There was fire and rain . . . and enough darkness for the Eadar who could still run to do so.' She retched and only then did Arturo put his hand on her arm to steady her.

'Rest for a time, Etaine,' said Cormac shortly. 'We will speak again later.'

Arturo helped her from the room but the moment the door had closed the small space erupted in the worst cursing Cormac had ever heard. Asgall's obscenities paused only for him to empty several mugs of mead but Beathan continued to storm around the room, cursing and slashing the air with his sword. Cormac remained where he was, hatred of Fada having congealed into a poisonous black core that rooted him to the spot.

'Why do you want to speak with her later?' demanded Asgall, chest heaving. 'Surely she has suffered enough?'

'There is a gap.'

Beathan gulped down more mead and wiped his chin. 'A gap?'

'Etaine left for Craith seven years ago and it was attacked five years ago come Bride's Day. Fionn confirmed Etaine and Arturo joined their band three years ago and Etaine herself told me she had been in the north three years. There is a gap of two years.'

'She and Arturo might have Ranged alone,' said Beathan.

Cormac shook his head. 'The northern bands know who Ranges in their territories.'

'You aren't suggesting she is a Fada spy, are you?' said Asgall incredulously. 'That she did not escape but was released?'

'I think Etaine and Lagan had a child.'

Asgall froze and Beathan sagged against the wall. 'Sweet Goddess,' he muttered.

There was a long silence and it was Cormac who broke it. 'We all know something is amiss with her and I won't risk the lives of my band by including a Ranger I cannot trust. I might be wrong about the child and I hope I am, but by night's end, I intend to know where those two missing years went.'

They re-joined the gathering, but none were in the mood for light-hearted chatter and the Rangers were beginning to drift away in any case. It had been a hard day of climbing and the next day would start early. Asgall and Beathan kept Cormac company but as the night deepened, they embraced him, and left him alone by the fire.

Cormac knew he must seek Etaine out again, but he dreaded it. He had told Asgall and Beathan he hoped Etaine and Lagan had not had a child and it was true, for he could scarcely bear to think of it being murdered in front of her, and yet it would explain so much of her behaviour. And the question remained as to whether she could overcome her hatred of Fada sufficiently to fight as a disciplined band-member, as his Rangers must.

The sky was ablaze with stars and he stared up at it, seeking his namesake, the *fitheach* star-pattern, and Etaine's namesake, the *lasair*: the shining flame. A great drift of stars separated the raven from the flame, but the star-patterns were closer in the heavens than he and Etaine were on the ground.

Cormac sighed and set off deeper into the oaks. Fire smoke made the camp easy to find but neither Etaine nor Arturo were there. The night's lateness meant they would not be far, and given Etaine's love of the Goddess, she at least was likely to be at the pool the guards reported lay upstream. He went on along the stream's sedge-lined bank and came to a stop where it kinked sideways to form a wide dish of water. Glow-flies clustered at his feet and starlight glittered the mist on the pool's surface.

Something white moved over the water and ripples glimned silver as they reached the shore. At first Cormac thought it was a swan and then he realised it was Etaine swimming. He remembered now she swam in all seasons, taking delight in her nearness to the Goddess. He knew he intruded but as she stepped from the water, the silhouette of her star-silvered body held him transfixed.

And then something slammed down across his throat, forced his head back, and cut off his air. He managed to get a hand to his knife, but a punishing blow smashed it from his grip. Whatever held him had the bulk of a bear and the cunning of a he- and Cormac's head swam with confusion and the need to breathe.

'Arturo! Release him. He has seen nothing he has not seen before.'

It was Etaine, but her voice was faint, as if it came from afar, and the crushing bar across his throat remained. 'Arturo!'

The bar was withdrawn and Cormac stumbled to his knees and sucked in air as he snatched up his knife. Arturo loomed over him, eyes yellow in the starlight, teeth barred and then he turned and lumbered off through the oaks. He was naked; his great arms furred; his back streaked with crushed moss.

Cormac struggled to his feet and by the time he had reached Etaine, she had donned her trousers and was buttoning her shirt. 'He is a shifter,' he said hoarsely, as he rubbed his throat.

'Aren't we all? Seeming one thing one day and something else the next.'

'Why is he with you?'

'He agreed,' she said, as she buckled on her wrist-knives and pulled on her boots.

'Agreed?'

'He was asked to be with me and he agreed.'

She picked up her jacket and went to pass him, but he fell into step beside her. 'Asked by whom?'

'Those who knew I needed him, I suppose.'

'So that was three years ago?'

'Yes.'

Etaine's words raised even more questions but he remained silent even after they reached her camp. She tossed more wood on the fire and settled beside it, but Cormac remained standing as he contemplated her. She had let the band *and* him think she and Arturo were mate-paired and the fact they were not, partly explained Arturo's lack of reaction to Cormac's questioning of her, although Arturo was certainly protective in bear-form. But none of it explained the gap in years.

'What is it you want, Toiseach?' Her voice was weary and she kept her gaze on the fire.

'I want to know what you were doing between Craith and returning to Ranging.'

'Recovering.'

'Two years is a long time to recover in, Etaine.'

She stood and turned her back and for a moment he thought she would storm off through the oaks but then he realised she unbuttoned her shirt. His guts knotted but nothing could have prepared him for the shock as she dropped the shirt below her shoulders. The scar radiated like a star-burst from her shoulder blades to halfway down her back in a series of hard white ridges and gouged flesh.

He had only ever seen such wounds on corpses and his knives were in his hands and every muscle tensed for battle before he realised it. Fada used the star-brand to drive the foul Eadar spirit back to its maker the Serpent, as if the brand replicated the purity of the stars. But the brand was a parody of all that was bright and beautiful in the world.

Etaine fastened her shirt and turned back to him, the fire-flames lighting the gaunt planes of her face. 'I can carry a pack all day if I walk, Toiseach, and half if I run, then Arturo carries it for me. I can climb as fast as any Ranger, but I use my legs more than my arms to push myself up. I cannot wield a sword or bow, for scar does not stretch like skin; I use knives instead. I am accurate and I am fast.'

There was a blur and a thwack as a knife embedded itself in the ground between his feet. She came to him and retrieved it. 'I am a strong member of your band, Toiseach. I won't fail you or them.'

'Etaine,' he said thickly, and ran his fingers gently down her cheek. The scent of her water-sweet skin filled his senses and then was replaced with emerald light as her she-Eadar spirit kindled his. He brought his mouth to hers unthinkingly, following where the emerald light led and in an instant, he was back with her under the oaks in Boath. It was as if a burning twig had fallen from a fire in that time and ignited a new understanding in this.

And then she wrenched herself free, chest heaving, her face a mask of pain and longing. 'I won't risk another Craith,' she said, and then in a voice that tore at his heart: 'You abandoned us.'

Cormac was adrift in a sea of emerald light and his brain grappled with all that had been revealed *and* concealed. It took a long time for the Light Way to fully return and when it did, it brought with it the weariness of the long day. He wanted time to think, not to argue with her again, and they would be leaving at dawn, heading into something that could be as bloody as Craith, but for Fada this time, he pledged.

'I thank you for sharing what happened at Craith,' he said formally. 'I know it was painful for you and I wish you Fair Dreams to soothe you this night.' Then with a low bow, he made his way back through the oaks.

16

The next morning Cormac breakfasted with the Cean-nards around the main fire while the Rangers not guarding gathered at the others. Thin streams of oak-scented smoke mixed with the last of the mist, but despite the chill, no one bothered to cart more fuel; they would depart as soon as they breakfasted.

They ate cold joints of boar and hare and yesterday's bread softened with meat juices; a feast compared to what they would hunt and forage on the journey, and which would be washed down with water, not mead. But no Ranger needed to be reminded the time of celebration was at an end.

Cormac discussed possible routes and campsites with the Ceannards but shared none of the strategies they might adopt in Lisanisk. The brutal truth remained that the less the Rangers knew, the less they could scream out under a star-brand's sear. Etaine's mutilation haunted him as did the possibility her child had been murdered but he forced his anger deep inside where he kept all Fada's loathsome activities.

The Ranger in him wanted to stab and slash Fada into oblivion regardless of the cost but the Toiseach knew de-

113

feating them would be no victory if Eadar numbers were decimated for years to come.

Given Etaine's description of Fada strategies at Craith, Cormac had formed his Rangers back into bands of fourteen. The bands would take different routes to Lisanisk to reconnoitre the springs and streams along the way but reunite beyond the settlement's walls and march in together.

Cormac had selected most of the members of each band but had asked the Ceannards to choose one or two Rangers who would lead if the Ceannard were injured or killed. He had chosen Asgall and Beathan for the purpose in his own band and had included Etaine and Arturo in the remaining twelve; a choice he would have to justify to Beathan, if not to Asgall.

Etaine and Arturo emerged from the oaks but he had known of Etaine's approach long before she appeared. Since he had kissed her last night, his dreams had been filled with emerald light and even now, in the early morning chill, the sense of wonderment remained.

The Emerald Way was a gift she had given him seven years ago and then withdrawn, and to walk there again was as heady as the sweetest draught of mead. And yet his heightened awareness also told him something was missing, or else he had missed something, which was not the same thing.

Etaine's claim of abandonment remained inexplicable but at least he knew she had not taken Lagan out of malice. The kiss had revealed anger and pain, big things like the oak's spreading branches, not small pinched things like meanness and spite, and Cormac knew the explanation he had concocted to make her desertion bearable was false.

The irony of what unfolded was not lost on him either. For seven years he had yearned for her return *and* for the return of the Emerald Way, and now she was back and in a single kiss had re-ignited a need for her as powerful as that in Boath.

But he was no longer an ordinary Ranger, free to take a mate at will. He was a Toiseach and facing a battle that might prove every bit as bloody as Craith. His whole focus must be on defeating Fada and that meant his own wants and needs must wait.

Asgall and Beathan were pleased with the band's make-up which consisted of Artair and Tormod for their speed; Raild, Rahg, Padair and Seumas for their sword and arrow skills; and Siomon, Ringean, Eion, Steaphan, Bress and Caitlin for their knowledge of Lisanisk and its surrounds. But, as Cormac had predicted, their disapproval of Etaine and Arturo's inclusion was clear.

His band spoke amongst themselves while they waited for him but Etaine and Arturo stood to one side and Cormac was not surprised by their exclusion, given they were the only northern Rangers. Yet it was crucial his Rangers acted as one, and Asgall and Beathan were vital in bringing that about.

He had Ranged with them since they had all left the east and they had shared his excitement at finding Etaine in Boath *and* celebrated his joy when she had chosen him as her mate, but it had also been left to them to pass on the news of her hand-fasting and departure. Beathan had been particularly scathing: *She sulked in her room for days after you left and then suddenly she is out and hand-fasted and gone. And not even the usual feast to mark the grand occasion.*

Cormac had churned Beathan's words over in his mind countless times but only now was he was struck by their oddness. Etaine had never chosen to sleep *inside*, even at Boath. He probably had not noticed the anomaly before because he had immediately thrown himself back into

Ranging, choosing the most dangerous and difficult tasks to dull the pain and pretend nothing was amiss. Asgall and Beathan had not been fooled though and they had laid the blame for his wounding squarely at Etaine's feet.

The first part of the route Cormac had chosen took his band back to the Drumin Crags but they had not gone far before he dropped back to the rear where Beathan and Asgall walked, and then slowed his steps until a gap opened between them and the rest of the Rangers.

'I found the two missing years,' he said, without preamble. 'Etaine spent them healing.'

'That is a long time to heal,' said Beathan gruffly.

'My sentiments exactly but then I have never known an Eadar to survive a star-brand before.'

Asgall's shock was clear and it even took Beathan a moment to recover. 'She told you she had been branded?' he asked.

'She showed me.' They walked in silence for a time and even the chaffinches seemed robbed of their voices. 'It explains why she cannot run with a pack for an entire day, use an arrow or sword, or haul herself up when she climbs,' continued Cormac. 'But she did give me a demonstration of her knife skills, which Asgall has already witnessed, and I believe she will still be an asset to our band.'

'Is that the only reason you have included her?' challenged Beathan.

'No. She brings Arturo with her and it is useful to have a shifter on your side.'

'A shifter?' exclaimed Asgall. 'When did you discover that?'

'Last night when he all but throttled me.'

'Upset him, did you?' asked Beathan dryly with a smile. Cormac smiled too, knowing Beathan's antagonism to Etaine had subsided.

'So, why is a shifter keeping company with a she-Eadar?' asked Asgall.

'He agreed to apparently. I am guessing he was asked to protect her but by whom and for what purpose, I do not know. Etaine does not know either. I will pursue that after Lisanisk. It would be useful to have more shifters working with us and against Fada,' he added thoughtfully.

'But unlikely,' said Asgall, and Cormac reluctantly agreed. Little was known of shifters except they kept to themselves and while they did not aid Fada, their reclusiveness did not aid Eadar either.

Cormac worked his way back up through his Rangers, surprised to see Arturo now walked with Bress, and Caitlin with Etaine. Caitlin had kept company with Isbeil but Isbeil was in Fionn's band following a more southerly route. Caitlin was keeping up a steady stream of chatter and while he noted Etaine did not join in, she nodded occasionally.

The Emerald Way bloomed about him as he approached her, and he had to concentrate on keeping his pace even as he moved past. But leaving Etaine behind, if only in the body of his band, was harder than he expected, and he wondered again at the power a single kiss had woken.

The wind freshened during the morning and by the time they reached the Drumin's foothills, Cormac had decided to take the gentler route he had used to descend yesterday. As well as being an easier climb, it provided shelter such as clefts and pine groves, should the weather turn stormy again. The last thing he needed was another fall like Etaine had suffered.

He led the climb, keeping the pace steady and an eye

on the clouds, and cursed silently as they darkened. He had learned how quickly sunshine gave way to rain and gusting winds in the peaks and sent word back to seek shelter. He continued, searching for clefts that opened to the skies.

The wind grew chill but he was so engrossed in solving the mystery of Etaine's fall, that the first crack of thunder caught him unawares and he swiftly doubled back to the last cleft he passed. Rain poured down as he scrambled inside and, as he shook the water from his jacket, he realised he was not alone.

The glories of the Emerald Way pulsed about him, still shadowy but so potent he had to steady himself against the wall. Etaine sat at the back of the cleft and he settled beside her, took her cool wet hand in his, and locked their fingers.

The rain sluiced down the stone outside but he no longer heard it for, deep in the Emerald Way, he saw an exquisite golden arc, fractured at its centre. It was the link they had seeded in Boath and every fibre of his being yearned for its completion, but then it was gone *and* the emerald vales, and he was back in the cleft, surrounded by the smell of wet stone.

Etaine prowled up and down inside the small space and he scrambled to his feet. 'You *have* to tell me,' he said. She continued to pace and he caught her arm. 'Tell me, Etaine!'

'The Emerald Way does not deal in words,' she said savagely, jerking herself free. 'You either see or you do not see; you are either sighted or you are blind!'

Blindness was a charge she had thrown at him more than once, but then she came to a stop and pushed her hand through her hair. 'Maybe the fault is mine,' she muttered, as if to herself. 'Maybe I imagined you were something you were not. Maybe I just chose poorly. But I won't risk it again, Cormac, not after Craith.'

Much of what she said was incomprehensible but of one thing he was certain. 'Our link *is* true,' he said. 'I felt it back in Boath but I have *seen* it now. I will give you whatever time you need, Etaine, and when you grant me the trust to tell me how I have wronged you, I will recompense you in whatever way I can, but I swear to you now that I will *never* lose you again.'

17

The storm dissipated quickly which suited Etaine. She did not want to risk being confined with Cormac again or worse still, come to believe his desertion at Boath could be undone. It had been a mistake to think his true-Eadar colouring reflected true-Eadar blood and yet … coming together with him again had revealed a link she had scarcely known existed. It was incomplete but it explained why he had haunted her for seven long years.

If only Fionn had kept them in the north! Then she would not have to deal with Cormac's demands as Toiseach *and* as a former mate! And now he could badger her in the Emerald Way too!

She seethed as she considered Cormac's pledge to *never lose her again*. He had not *lost* her in the first place; he had *abandoned* her *and* their unborn child, and such was his blindness *and* arrogance, he thought he could simply step back into her life.

But as much as Cormac infuriated her, the link made him impossible to ignore, as did his he-Eadar potency. He might not have been the true-mate she had searched for but his kiss last night and touch today were like the Goddess's sweet rains on parched earth, and she wondered briefly whether she could join with him without consequence or commitment as she had planned to join with Taig. But Cormac was no young he-Eadar to be taken when it suited her and cast aside, and he had staked his claim.

Cormac did not speak to her for the rest of the day, which was a relief, in fact, he did not even walk near her, but the link that had drawn him into the Emerald Way caused a subtle shift in the Light Way too that the Rangers sensed. Eadar felt Eadar connections in the Emerald Way despite being unable to consciously Remember it and Etaine caught Beathan and Asgall's gazes upon her, *and* Bress's too, whose chestnut hair and pale eyes belied his sensitivity.

Arturo continued to keep Bress company and Etaine wondered if he distanced himself from her in preparation for his departure. Whatever his motivations, it left the place at her side empty and Caitlin wasted no time in filling it, or in sharing her thoughts.

'It is said you have renewed your coupling with the Toiseach,' she said bluntly. 'Some of the Rangers fear you will distract him or he will focus on keeping you safe rather than leading us. Others fear Arturo will confront him or refuse to fight.'

Etaine's first instinct was to stay silent but that might damage band unity. 'Do you fear Isbeil will be hurt or killed when the fighting starts?' she asked instead.

'Of course,' said Caitlin.

'Are you going to ignore the rest of us and fight only for her?'

'Of course not. I am fighting for the Eadar.'

'All the Rangers are fighting for the Eadar, Caitlin, including Arturo and the Toiseach. I saw what Fada did

121

in Craith and the Toiseach knows too. He is focussed on scouring their murdering taint from the land, as we all are.'

Caitlin let the topic be but Etaine realised her response had cleared her own mind and that her link with Cormac in the Emerald Way was irrelevant to what lay ahead. She was one of seventy-five Rangers going to Lisanisk to prevent Fada repeating Craith's slaughter and that was all that mattered.

They were about half way up Cairn Toul when Cormac turned off the path and led them west across a stony saddle of land that divided Cairn Toul from the neighbouring peak of Cairn Dearg. By midday, they had begun their descent. The land was kinder on the Drumin's western slopes with stands of lime, elm and hazel joining the pine, and the cries of jays and siskins mixing with those of chaffinches.

The Drumin's height gave a good view west and as they followed the winding path down, Etaine gazed towards where Lisanisk must lie. Caitlin had told her Lisanisk was walled and Etaine recalled how Fada had used Craith's walls to shut them in and their rescuers out.

The prospect of being confined with Fada again brought her out in a cold sweat.

She would be unable to strike from the cover of trees then slip away to kill again. She would have to pass them in Lisanisk's stone streets; feel their blank grey eyes appraise her; see their lips draw back from their perfect teeth in what they called smiles. And it would not end there. She would have to share food in taverns; drink from the same wells; and every moment of every day, risk a spear or sword thrust in the back.

It was dusk before they reached the valley floor, but they

did not make camp until the night had turned. Etaine was weary but glad they went on to the shelter of a forest. It was known as Ladhar Woods, according to Caitlin, and Siomon, who walked just behind them and whose kin still lived in the surrounding lands, said it had once been the haunt of Fuaran.

Etaine certainly thought the trees had a Fuaran feel about them, as did the spring they passed with its stands of juniper and collar of lady-fern. It fed a stream that meandered down over stonier ground and the band laid their bedrolls beside it, where the stone gave way to the softness of leaf-fall.

The nearness of the Goddess eased Etaine's tension as did Cormac's caution. He had sent Beathan and Raild ahead to reconnoitre and hunt, so by the time the remainder of the band arrived, pine martens and squirrels were roasting over a single fire. Cormac posted guards too and then went on scout, taking Bress with him.

Asgall oversaw the meal and ensured that once the meat was cooked and portioned, the fire was extinguished, the ashes and animal bones buried, and the detritus smoothed back into place. Having crossed the Drumins and trekked deep into the night, the Rangers were quick to sleep and Etaine was tired too, but sleep refused to come. She knew better than to stay in her bedroll, for lying wakeful in the darkness invited memories of Craith that would rob her of rest for days to come.

Arturo's bedroll remained untouched and as she set off back towards the spring, she wondered whether he guarded or replenished his spirit in natural form. How must it be to change shape at will? Had she been a bird-shifter she might have carried Ellair far from Fada knives and ropes.

Bloodied memories threatened and desperate for distraction, she clambered up the nearest pine in search of the stars. Before Craith she had scaled trees as swiftly as she had run but not anymore. She toiled on and when the trunk tapered, braced herself against it and scanned the sky. Her star-pattern was there as was Cormac's and she knew as Bride's Day neared, the *lasair* and *fitheach* would draw closer together. It was one of the things that had convinced her naïve eighteen-year-old self that Cormac was her true-mate.

She had learned hard lessons since then, the most brutal being to never again give Fada such power over her. Etaine cursed as her stomach resumed its churn. She had climbed the pine to clear her head, not carry the blackness up the tree with her!

The night-shrouded lands stretched away all about her and as she scanned a flick of orange caught her eye. A campfire, away to the south, but was it Adam's folk, another band's, or Fada? She estimated it was close to a day's travel off but she had no idea of the routes the other bands followed.

A bird scythed overhead and she flinched. A hooded-crow, its head and chest the same lifeless grey as the carcasses it fed from and flying in the fire's direction. But even as Etaine stared after it, the fire winked out. Adam's folk saw auguries in the smash of a wren's egg tossed from a nest but Eadar took note of their senses instead and the hair stirred on the back of her neck.

She climbed back down into the forest's gloom and wiped her sweaty hands on her trousers. She wished Arturo was with her but even if he were, what was she to say? I have seen a campfire and a hooded-crow flew past? I fear Fada are abroad with swords wet with Eadar blood?

It was indeed what she feared but she wondered whether the fear flowed from her memories of Craith. She quickened her steps, hungry for the Goddess's solace and, nodding to Tormod who guarded nearby, pushed her way through the junipers to the spring. It was even darker within their shelter and she started as a toad hopped clear.

The spring's seep was too slow to carry the Goddess's voice and Etaine's sense of foreboding returned. The campfire had probably been Adam's folk, she told herself, either herding their animals or in search of lynx or squirrel for the pot, but the explanation rang hollow

Something moved on the edge of her vision and, in one smooth motion, she dropped into a crouch and flung a belt-knife then grimaced. She had killed the toad.

'Better the *losgann* than me,' said Cormac, as he stepped from the junipers. He cleaned her knife on the lady-fern and handed it back. 'Tormod told me you were here but you should be sleeping. It is another long day tomorrow.' Etaine said nothing and Cormac's tone lightened. 'And how does the Goddess this night?'

'She is silent.'

'Maybe *She's* sleeping,' he said, and moved nearer.

His potent he-Eadar scent enveloped Etaine and her heart quickened as his mouth came to hers. Hungry for comfort, she did not pull away and as their kiss deepened, she wondered again whether she could snatch a brief hiatus of pleasure before Lisanisk's horror began.

In the Emerald Way, the halves of their golden link drew nearer, close enough now for him to sense her fear and his attention shifted. 'You are frightened, Etaine. Why?'

'I climbed a pine to see the stars and saw a fire to the south. A day's travel, I guess.'

'Were you looking for trouble?'

It was a question only one true-Eadar would ask of another but Etaine did not know how to answer. Sleep had not come and she had climbed out of the trees' darkness and seen a fire her heart told her was Fada. 'I was not looking for trouble, but I think I have found it,' she said.

'It could be Fionn's band; it fits with his route, but

Fionn knows better than to light a fire in the open. If you saw it, Fada could too.'

If Cormac feared Fada had already found Fionn's band, he gave no sign of it, simply took her hand, and escorted her back to where the others slept.

'I wish you sleep and Fair Dreams,' he said solemnly, then kissed her palm and turned to his own bedroll.

Etaine *did* sleep but her dreams were far from fair. She dreamed the spring began to bubble, not the gentle silvery bubbles of the Goddess's breath, but the violent ructions putrefying swamps sometimes belched. And as Etaine looked down into the spring, the bodies of Fionn and the others of his band; white, eyeless, and mutilated, had one by one been vomited to the surface.

18

Arturo did not return to camp until close to dawn and then it was with a scratched face and a body that reeked of sweat. It did not matter. Etaine pulled her bed-roll close and curled up in the shelter of his body. He did not ask why and nor had he ever, just brought his arm over her. Early in their time together, Etaine could not sleep unless some part of her rested against him, and even now, his touch had the power to keep the worst of her dreams at bay.

Light filtered through the branches, but she kept her eyes shut and tried to think only of the shifter at her back. The soft footfalls of Rangers told her the band had roused and she knew Cormac had risen too, not because she heard him in quiet conversation with Asgall, but because she sensed him in the Emerald Way.

Arturo slept on but Etaine reluctantly opened her eyes. The little of the sky she could see was grey and the air felt damp. She sat up, rolled her stiff shoulders, and took a long draught from her waterskin. Caitlin smiled as she passed but Etaine's sense of dread made it hard to smile back.

No one else seemed affected; their voices kept low out

of habit rather than dread and she pondered again whether her unease flowed from thoughts of Fada. Since Craith their blank stares had haunted her dreams and she wondered whether their mates and children shared the same stone-hard gazes. She would never know. The he-Fada had left those *they* loved behind, safe in the lands they had sailed from.

Cormac did not approach her until they were about to set off and he had Bress with him. Bress knew the surrounding lands well and Cormac wanted her to describe exactly where she had seen the fire.

'It sounds like Riamh Wood,' said Bress, when Etaine had fallen silent. 'Not a place Fada favour. Too many demons,' he added dryly. Etaine nodded, familiar with Fada's hatred of forests, especially oak forests. The oaks' broad branches trapped the scent of the Goddess's sweet sap, pulled from the deep by the trees' massive roots and, according to Fada, poisoned the air with the foulness of the Serpent that lurked beneath.

'We will detour south to investigate,' said Cormac, 'and if we find nothing, return to our original route. I do not want the bands travelling too closely together.'

Etaine contemplated all the things Cormac *had not* said, as she walked, such as what they would do if they *did* find something. Dead Fada would mark a Ranger victory and dead Rangers a Fada one and more troublingly, prove Fada frequented places they had previously shunned.

The heavy clouds added to Etaine's sense of oppression but despite her minimal responses, Caitlin was her usual talkative self. 'You do not speak much, do you?' she said after a while. 'Neither does Arturo. I suppose that is what makes you a good mate-pair.'

'We are not a mate-pair,' said Etaine, sensing Arturo would soon leave and not wanting him accused of desertion.

'Oh. I guess that explains the Toiseach then.'

'We are not a mate-pair either.'

Caitlin glanced sideways at her. 'It is said you were in Boath.'

'Boath was a long time ago.'

'Time is irrelevant in the Emerald Way,' said Caitlin, her eyes on the sky. 'Looks like we are in for rain again.'

Etaine all but stumbled. Caitlin was right! In the Emerald Way it was as if she and Cormac had just coupled and their link's completion waited only on Cormac's return. It was why the link strengthened with his every touch and why even his proximity fed it! But their link could never be as the Serpent demanded.

Coupling had made them one and the Emerald Way had opened to them; and Ellair's seeding had made them three and Etaine had briefly entered the Serpent Way, but then Cormac's abandonment had locked her out.

And while she Remembered enough to receive the gifts the Emerald Way offered the Serpent Way remained closed to her. The exclusion of lesser-Eadar was even greater. Those who coupled might Remember enough to speak of the Emerald Way but never walk there. It remained hidden from them like the Serpent Way, sensed as the sun is when obscured by clouds, but never to be seen.

If Adam's folk had been as hard and hungry as Fada, there would be more true-Eadar but Adam's folk had been as gentle with the Eadar as they were with the land, and so children had been seeded with blood robbed of Remembering. The horror of how blindly Eadar had slipped into the Unremembered and the consequences for Ellair, swamped her and she staggered.

Caitlin grabbed her arm. 'Are you unwell?'

Cormac led but strode back and Etaine realised even their incomplete link gave him an instant awareness of her state. He clipped out orders for a rest break then led her away from the band and held his waterskin to her mouth. The cool slide of water down her throat brought the smell of the Light Way's wet earth and she steadied.

'Something is amiss with you Etaine,' he said tersely, 'and I need to what it is. I need to know whether I can rely on you once the fighting starts.'

'You can rely on me, Toiseach.'

'That is for me to judge,' he said, with the harshness of a leader who has discovered a fatal flaw in his battle plan.

'I used to vomit when I thought of Craith. Now I just feel ill.'

Cormac's anger at her branding reverberated through the Emerald Way but his face betrayed nothing. 'That will affect your ability to fight in Lisanisk.'

'It is different when Fada are near. Then I want only to kill. You can confirm that with Asgall, Toiseach.'

'I have. But in Lisanisk, we fight as a band. Will you be able to control your hatred enough for that?'

Cormac spoke as a Toiseach must, but the Emerald Way told a very different story and Etaine struggled to reconcile the two. Deceit was alien to Eadar but so too was deserting your mate and child and she was in no mood to make excuses for him. His eyes burned with an angry flame but Etaine looked full into them and felt the jolt she delivered in the emerald lands.

'I am waiting for your answer, Etaine.'

'I will be able to control my hatred as much as you will be able to control yours.'

Her words told him she was aware of his want to avenge her branding and the lines around his mouth deepened. 'Beathan warned me of this complication,' he said.

'There is no complication, Toiseach. I will kill as many Fada in Lisanisk as I can, as will you and the band.'

'Yes, but unlike the rest of us, I do not sense you want to survive. That is the complication, Etaine, for your survival is the most important thing in the world to me.'

His face now matched her sense of him in the Emerald Way and Etaine felt the halves of their link reach out to each other as a leaf unfolds, sweet with the flow of new sap. Almost she believed things could be undone; that the scars on her back could be unmade; that Ellair could be returned to life but then the Light Way's brutal reality slammed home.

'Do not waste your time on me, Toiseach,' she said. 'I died at Craith. I am simply waiting for my heart to stop.'

19

Cormac led his band out of the trees and south over the tussocky plains. Rain misted down but he kept them at a fast pace, keen to reach Riamh Woods. The lands they crossed were favoured by Adam's folk for their animals *and* by mounted Fada, and his tension built as the trees' shelter receded. He sensed his Rangers' tension rise too. Etaine marched at the back near Asgall and Beathan and he half wished he *had* left her behind in Ballindalloch's safely, *if* it were safe.

Asgall and Beathan had voiced no more objections to her presence but he knew their concerns remained, as his did. Everything told him she needed time away from fighting to heal, but time was the one thing he could not offer her, not with the approach of Bride's Day. He still had no idea of Fada intentions, beyond them being murderous, and he wondered abruptly if the Emerald Way could aid him.

Etaine had used it against Fada when she had hidden their corpses and while the emerald vales remained indistinct, he sensed they would be clearer once his link with Etaine was complete, and it *would* complete, despite her antagonism.

Etaine's presence was strong in the Emerald Way which suggested that, seven years ago in Boath, she had Remembered when he had not. His heart quickened as he wondered whether that was the source of her anger and pain. *You abandoned us:* was the *us* the Emerald Way and not the rest of the band as he had supposed? But it did not fit with her familiarity with its emerald lands. Perhaps she referred to the Serpent Way. It had been there too at their joining, but he could not recall *how* or *why*, in fact, it was a struggle to even consider it, and yet the idea that the Serpent or Emerald Way could aid him persisted.

As the rain grew heavier, the harsh realities of the Light Way returned with a vengeance, and his attention swung back to what they might find at Riamh Wood. He could not ignore Etaine's heightened sensibilities but unless he saw evidence that Fionn's band had been attacked, he would have to assume his plans to reunite with them and the other bands at Cranoch Forest remained intact.

It was certainly quicker journeying over open land and given Fionn's route had been this way, the fire could have been theirs, *or* Adam's folk's *or* Fada. The dark edge of Riamh Wood grew closer, smudged over by the rain, and Cormac sent Raild and Ringean ahead on scout.

Ringean was the first to jog back, his face grim. 'Lots of fresh cut earth, Toiseach,' he said, 'and horse waste.'

'How many horses?' asked Cormac.

Ringean's brows drew low over his emerald eyes. 'More than ten but probably less than twenty. They ran together and then broke, some going east and others west in an arc. I did not scout further to see if they regrouped.'

It was a common Fada manoeuvre of encirclement, but Cormac kept his face expressionless while he waited for Raild's return but Raild reported nothing unusual.

Mounted Fada heading to Lisanisk would not have camped at Riamh Wood; it was too close to the comforts of Comlin and Lach's taverns, but it would be a different story if they were on hunt. And even had there been only ten of them, they would have the advantage over fifteen Eadar, on foot, in the open.

Ringean's news rippled through the band and the Rangers strode on stony-faced; none deluding themselves that mounted Fada augured well. As Riamh Wood's oaks emerged from the rain, Cormac ordered his band to fan out and jog, knowing a single running Ranger made a more difficult target than a close-packed, slow moving group. A great cloud of hooded-crows rose at their approach, their cries like metal against stone, and it was Caitlin who ran on the flank who reached their feasting-site first.

She dropped to her knees and buried her face in her hands and Cormac sprinted the last of the way and slewed to a stop. For a moment he did not know what he looked at and then horror burned through him like acid. Fionn's band, mutilated with the star-brand, and laid out in a star-pattern, head to head, eyeless sockets staring at the sky.

Etaine had her arms around Caitlin but the she-Eadar had collapsed over Isbeil's body and her keening had joined the crows' harsh cries. Cormac stared up at their circling and wondered if he had made a fatal mistake. He had broken his band of seventy-four to reconnoitre the waters around Lisanisk, but he had also thought it safer to travel in smaller groups.

Seventy-five Rangers beyond the gaze of Adam's folk might just tempt Fada into a single murderous attack. Apart from the *benefits* of eliminating so many true-Eadar in a single strike, it would have the advantage of leaving the true-Eadar who visited Lisanisk for Bride's Day totally unprotected.

The encounter between Fionn's band and the mounted Fada might have been accidental, but it might also have been part of a Fada strategy. And if it were? The lands around Lisanisk might be strewn with the grotesque corpse-stars of the Rangers who had trusted Cormac to lead them. And he would not know how many of his Rangers had survived until they reached Cranoch Forest, two days away, *if* they reached it.

Beathan and Asgall came to his side and listened grim-faced as he shared his thoughts.

'We must hope it was an evil accident and plan for the fact it was not,' said Asgall. 'And it would be best to keep to the trees for the rest of the journey.'

Cormac nodded but the problem remained as to what to do with their slain comrades. The bands carried nothing to dig graves and yet the dead could not be left as an obscene parody of Bride or as a meal for the crows. In the days Unremembered, cairns were built over the dead, but he could ill afford the time and labour the task would cost them.

His Rangers waited in silence for some sign from him, Etaine and Arturo amongst them. Etaine still had her arms around Caitlin and while the she-Eadar had stopped her keening, her grief was palpable.

Cormac beckoned Etaine who passed Caitlin into Bress's care and made her way over.

'A cairn must be built over the dead,' he said softly. 'Would Arturo aid us in bear-form to collect stone? We cannot afford to linger.'

Etaine nodded but as she turned to go he caught her arm. 'Did you see this?'

Her face was beaded with rain and her emerald eyes intense in the grey light. 'I dreamed that Fionn's band was dead, mutilated as they are here, but they were in Lisanisk, in the Goddess's spring.'

'The Emerald Way warned you?'

Etaine hesitated. 'It sometimes allows a greater seeing.'

'Do you sense Fada have set a trap for us in Lisanisk?'

'Yes.'

He let her go and watched her talk with Arturo and the shifter move off into the trees, then she came back. 'Arturo will gather stone but he is not to be watched. We are to place the dead close to the trees and cover them with branches.'

Cormac nodded. 'How is Caitlin?'

'As we all are: lessened by the deaths of so many of our blood.'

Cormac considered Etaine's words as he supervised the grim task of shifting bodies. Eadar did not fear the dead but the number of slain was so distressing Cormac sensed a shift in the Emerald Way, as if a stone had smashed into a pool here in the Light Way and caused a ripple there.

A Ranger brought Cormac the signe as each body was laid in place and as Cormac packed them away, he grimly wondered how many more he would collect before Lisanisk was over with.

He helped cover the bodies with oak boughs but as he paced about on the edge of the trees, waiting for Arturo's return, he came across the charred animal bones. Fada had feasted in celebration of their slaughter, he realised in disgust. The only consolation was that Etaine had seen their fire and the Rangers had been warned, although it might be too late. If he had kept them together . . . He cut the thought off. He must learn from his mistakes not dwell on them, especially at the expense of the here and now.

When Arturo returned, Cormac led his Rangers to where the stone was, and while no one questioned where such a convenient pile had come from, some Rangers eyed Arturo speculatively. But even with Arturo's aid, it was dusk before the cairn was finished. It could not be helped; the slain must be honoured *and* protected.

Etaine came to him as they rested after the last stones had been laid in place. 'Are you to speak the Goddess's blessing before we go?' she asked.

'*Speak* Her blessing?' The dead were offered the blessing of the Goddess's water, not Her words and he knew of none. He wondered briefly if Etaine intended to highlight his ignorance of the Emerald Way, but her face bore no signs of it.

'I will show you while the band collects water,' she said.

Cormac tersely ordered his Rangers to fill their waterskins from the stream at the trees' margin and followed Etaine in the opposite direction but she did not go far before she stopped in the lee of an ancient oak that hid them from view.

Then she turned and took his face in her hands. 'What …' he began.

'Open yourself, Cormac,' she ordered, and with shocking suddenness he was in the Emerald Way. Nor was the abruptness of the change the only thing that stunned him; the misty veils had been ripped away and he reeled as he saw the imprint of the star-brand on her spirit and then, astonishingly, felt the soft flick of Fionn's band as they moved past. He glimpsed the glint of serpent scales too and then he was wrenched back to the Light Way, so dizzy he gripped the oak to stay upright.

'How long have you seen truly in the Emerald Way?' he demanded, raw from what she had revealed.

'Since we coupled.'

'Why take *me* there when you despise what we shared?'

'Because you blame yourself for the loss of Fionn's band, Toiseach, and I need to remind you the Light Way is not the only Way where we dwell. Remember the others but keep your thoughts here, where Eadar most need you.'

Her eyes burned with the same light as in the Emerald Way and his want of her flared. 'And where do *you* most need me, Etaine?' She hesitated, and he was reminded of Arturo's warning she might lie under threat. But what was the threat? That she would reveal what kept them apart?

'I need you where I have always needed you,' she replied, and that told him nothing at all.

20

Cormac kept his band moving well into the night. He wanted to make up for lost time but he also wanted to delay the grief that would beset them once they took to their bedrolls. They would have nothing to think of then but their friends' mutilated bodies and the pace he set would gift them the swift oblivion of an exhausted sleep.

At least his words seemed to have offered comfort, especially to Caitlin, and he could thank Etaine for granting him the Remembering to deliver them: *Eadar dwell where we have always dwelt: in the Light Way, in the Emerald Way, and in the Serpent Way. We remain undivided as the Goddess's spring, stream, and river are undivided. We remain one.* Then the Rangers had offered the cairn the Goddess's water, as they would have offered it to a single Eadar, the wetness silvering the cairn so that it shone in the last of the dying light.

Cormac sensed the band's hatred for Fada escalate as they walked but he knew it would serve them ill unless he channelled it into a cohesive strategy, and to do that, he needed to understand Fada plans. He needed to understand Etaine too because she seemed to hold the key to so much that might aid them, such as the Emerald Way.

Not only could she take him there but she had restored his Remembering so that he saw it as she did, in all its gleaming beauty. He had even glimpsed the Serpent. He groped after the memory but the more he pursued its glittering scales, the more indistinct they grew, and he reluctantly gave up and turned his attention to Etaine and Arturo.

Arturo puzzled him almost as much as Etaine. Shifters remained aloof and yet he had been with Etaine for three whole years. And then there were the Fuaran. They were so elusive many believed they had quit the Eadar's lands altogether and yet they had aided Etaine on Cairn Toul. Why were the shifters and Fuaran so keen to keep Etaine alive? Was it because she could access the Emerald Way? Even the Serpent Way? But to what purpose?

Cormac's frustration grew at how little headway he made but his newfound acuity in the Emerald Way told him Boath was an important part of the puzzle. He had trawled over Boath's events countless times but he did so again in the hope of some fresh insight.

Lagan had pursued Etaine in the lead up to Bride's Day, as had Donal, but Cormac had not considered them serious rivals. That had been a mistake *unless* Etaine had taken them as lovers while he was in Inschbain. It fitted with her intention to couple with Taig a few short days earlier but the whole notion rang false.

Despite Taig's true-Eadar colouring, Etaine had shown no interest in him until *after* Cairn Toul. Cormac paused. The wonder of finding her alive had wiped the rest of the day from his mind but now he examined it in meticulous detail. His own behaviour brought him no credit, but he pushed on and came to a stop at the pine grove where he had found her. There was something about the way she had looked at him then that reverberated in the Emerald Way even now. She had wanted to make peace with him, he perceived for the first time, or at least end their hostilities, and when he had ignored the offer, she had turned to Taig.

Cormac conceded he had been guilty of blindness on Cairn Toul but he certainly had not abandoned her in Boath and yet the charge remained a barrier to everything he craved and more crucially, he sensed, to defeating Fada.

He called a halt when they reached the stream-bounded grove of oaks Bress had told him of. Cormac was glad of the grove for while nothing could undo the day's horror, the Goddess's watery voice and the oaks' mighty branches drew the band closer to the shelter of the Emerald Way.

They set fires, for the oaks masked smoke, but there was little risk of attack so deep in the trees and by the time the fires were well alight, Arturo had returned from up-stream with trout for their meal. He carried them impaled on an arrow, but his wet hair suggested he had fished with teeth and claws.

Cormac posted guards and took the first shift with Caitlin. If she blamed him for Isbeil's death he wanted to give her the chance to vent her anger in private, and if not, to ease her grief by speaking of her friend. He found a small rise with good cover at their back and set an arrow. Caitlin did the same and as the night grew older, she spoke of Isbeil, as he hoped she would.

'Isbeil wanted to seed a child this spring,' she said softly, 'but Cian believed his true-Eadar blood made it too dangerous. No one knows how the fighting will turn in Lisanisk *or* afterwards, and Cian worried they would be separated.'

'She would be protected by other Rangers,' said Cormac, wondering whether Cian's confidence in his leader-ship was so low he feared for his mate in his absence.

'That would not be enough.'

'I know she-Eadar prefer to be with the father of their child early on but …'

'*Have* to be with them or risk death,' corrected Caitlin. 'Cian's true-Eadar remember.'

The trees roared about Cormac, although his eyes told him they were still, and he was blasted by a sense of urgency so powerful he had raised his bow before he realised both sensations came from the Emerald Way.

'Isbeil carried a lot of Adam's blood but Cian still worried he would not be there to sustain her spirit when the child first fed,' continued Caitlin. 'I think they should have taken the risk and had the joy of a child, and now it is too late.'

Caitlin's voice was all but drowned out by a Remembering that stormed through Cormac like a winter flood. He found it difficult to breathe, let alone speak and it was Caitlin who broke the silence. 'I beg your pardon, Toiseach. I did not intend to question your leadership and nor did Cian. It is natural he would fear the loss of his true-mate and unborn child.'

Cormac nodded and turned away as if intent on some threat beyond the oaks, but in truth he saw nothing; consumed by the catastrophic consequences of his absence in Inschbain. *You abandoned us.* And as Etaine weakened, she had stayed in her rooms until as death threatened, she had hand-fasted to Lagan. But Lagan had taken her to Craith where she had been mutilated and *his* child murdered. No wonder the Emerald Way was awash with her anger and pain and in the Light Way, she could scarcely bear to look at him.

Caitlin seemed content to guard in silence and the night was only disturbed by the owls' hunt for bats in the canopy, until Bress and Siomon relieved them and he escorted Caitlin back to the camp. Those not guarding slept, except for Etaine, who sat with her gaze on the fire.

He sat next to her, but did not touch her, just stared into the flames as she did. 'What did you name him?' he asked hoarsely. 'Or was it her? What did you name our child?' Etaine did not move but the Emerald Way reverberated as if struck by bolts. 'Tell me! I have a right to know.'

'You have *no* rights!'

'You should have told me there in Boath.' It sounded like an accusation though he did not intend it to be.

'You should have known!'

'Yes. I should have known,' he said bitterly. 'But all I felt was the wonder of having you. I was so dazzled by you I was blind to all else. I thought I had time to rid the Light Way of Fada and time to celebrate it; that the Light and Emerald Ways would be as they were when I had left, filled with the glory of your presence.' He caught her hand. 'I want it back, Etaine. I want you and the chance of another child.'

'I won't risk it!'

'*Everything* we do now is risk!' He dragged in a lungful of air and lowered his voice. 'We know our link yearns for completion; that we might move between the Ways as our forebears did; that the Ways might help us defeat Fada.'

She wrenched her hand free and scrambled upright, and he rose too. 'You were not at Craith! I will *never* give Fada that kind of power over me again!'

Cormac caught her hand again and tightened his grip as she tried to pull away. 'We need to talk,' he said, and led her away upstream to where the stonier bed gave the water a voice he hoped would soothe her. But the water sounded discordant even to his own ears and the reverberations in the Emerald Way continued unabated.

'I guarded with Caitlin,' he said, 'and she spoke of how Isbeil had wanted a child and of Cian's reluctance. Cian had Remembered the fatal risk of separation and then

I Remembered.

'Too late!'

'Yes. Too late to save you from what happened in Craith; too late to save our child.'

The pain of the revelation surged through him anew and her hand convulsed in his as the halves of their link pulsed with golden light. 'Ellair,' she said raggedly. 'I called him Ellair.'

'Ellair,' repeated Cormac. 'What was he like?'

'Like you.'

'And what of Lagan? Did he know?'

'Lagan wanted me and so he took Ellair. He treated Ellair as his own, loved him as his own but we never spoke of it.' She ran a shaking hand through her hair. 'I won't risk another child, Cormac.'

'But will you risk me?' He regretted the question the moment it left his lips. It gave her the opportunity to end his hopes once and for all, but blessedly, the tumult in the Emerald Way subsided.

'It is the same thing.'

'It does not have to be. Love wears many faces.' He drew her into his arms, relieved she did not resist, and as he held her, it seemed he still lay with her under the oaks at Boath, afire with the intoxicating potency of their union. Waves of Remembering surged through him and in the Emerald Way, the two halves of their link flared brighter than flame.

Etaine broke away but Cormac barely noticed, overcome with all that had been revealed. 'It is as if I never left,' he gasped in wonderment. 'As if the last seven years never existed. The need to be with you, to be with … Ellair … is overwhelming.' He struggled to steady. 'I do not understand why I did not Remember then as you did. Etaine … I cannot undo the wrong. I cannot bring our child back but … for us to turn away from each other, for *Eadar* to refuse to couple for fear of what Fada will do to our children, is to hand our futures to them without stringing bows or drawing swords. Their victory will be absolute.

'Coupling makes us vulnerable but it also makes us strong,' he continued urgently. 'When we join, we walk the Emerald Way and might even enter the Serpent Way as in the days Unremembered. Since you have come back, since you have *allowed* me back, I have felt the power there. It is a power we can use against the Fada.'

'I *won't* risk it!'

'You have told me what happened in Craith and we have seen the start of Lisanisk's bloodshed today. The Fada will have learned from Craith, as we have. Whatever they intend at Lisanisk will be different but no less deadly. For us to survive it, for *Eadar* to survive *at all*, we must risk it!'

'No!' Her distress was clear, and Cormac forced himself to calm.

'Now is not the time to discuss it, not on this day of death,' he said more quietly, 'but Fada swords await in Lisanisk and Eadar there depend on us for protection, so *if* you do choose to risk it, it *must* be soon.'

Etaine and Cormac were oblivious to the owl perched in the branches above them and it remained there until the dawn-silvered air glimned the antlers of a stag, and then the owl glided down and settled nearer the ground. A she-Fuaran's reflection joined the owl and stag's on the stream's bright surface, but while their images wavered, the Fuaran's remained unchanged.

'The he-Eadar has Remembered,' said the Fuaran.

'And being he-Eadar, thinks of how the Serpent might serve him,' said the stag.

'He thinks too much and feels too little,' said the owl,

its voice taking on the cadences of its other self.

'He feels more now,' said the Fuaran. 'He knows the loss of his child and his failings.'

'It is a beginning,' conceded the owl.

'But not an ending,' said the stag. 'For that he must join with the she-Eadar.'

'They have joined before; we know they are true,' said the Fuaran.

'He must first regain her trust,' said the owl, 'and I wonder if we have healed her enough for that.' On the water's surface, its head drooped and the Fuaran's reflection moved closer.

'There comes a time when fawns must run and hatchlings fly,' said the Fuaran soothingly.

'Yet time is short,' said the owl. 'Even the Goddess is uneasy.'

'We are so close,' said the stag, the stars catching its eyes as it tossed its head. 'But only Arturo can follow beyond the walls and his task is not ours. What of the Fuaran?'

'The Fuaran serve the Serpent as we have always done. We wait to see if the shining one and raven Remember that they must serve the Serpent too.'

21

C ormac kept the band within the oaks' deep shelter for the next part of the journey, but the trees' emerald light did nothing to soothe Etaine. Life had been simple when she only had to kill and survive to kill again, but Cormac wanted her to seed another child with him and then presumably, somehow keep it and herself alive.

She fumed at his arrogance as she strode along beneath the oaks' spreading branches. He might finally have understood the full depths of his betrayal but he had no understanding *at all* of what he now demanded of her! And while it was true the Eadar's refusal to couple *would* hand victory to Fada, Cormac deluded himself if he thought *their* coupling could undo Craith's slaughter. The Emerald Way was separate to the Light Way, and in the Light Way, there was no going back.

Etaine walked on her own, glad Caitlin had chosen to keep Bress company, and Arturo was ahead with Beathan, which reinforced her belief Arturo prepared her for his departure. He still set his bedroll next to hers each night and held her when she needed comfort, but he was increasingly aloof during the day.

Given the toll of holding an unnatural shape for so

long, she did not think it had been shifters who had asked him to stay with her, which left the Fuaran. It had been Fuaran who had retrieved her from Craith, who had tended her after her fall from Cairn Toul, who had shown her the blasted pine that had told her, with a clarity that needed no words, that she too could heal and birth new life. Perhaps that particular she-Fuaran was friends with Cormac! But it begged the question *why* the Fuaran had bothered with her at all.

In Craith, Fada had focused their murderous attentions on true-Eadar first and Etaine had been amongst the last to be dealt with. She had no idea how many true-Eadar had escaped that night *or* lesser-Eadar for that matter, because by the time the Hall was burning, she was beyond knowing anything at all.

Memories of Craith roused the usual nausea and Cormac was aware of it in the Emerald Way, just as she was aware of his hatred and want for revenge. Subterfuge was impossible there which was why he had no need to ask whether her desire for him endured. But seven hard years had left her scarred inside and out, and with choices that had narrowed down to selecting the best way to kill.

Cormac hoped the Serpent's realm would provide a weapon to defeat Fada but she had learned long ago that hope was as amorphous as her glimpse of the Serpent, whereas in the Light Way, the Fada were as hard and sharp as their swords.

Cormac spoke to Etaine rarely in the days that followed, but his gaze was on her often and in the Emerald Way, his attention was unrelenting. She resented his intrusion there *and* his demands which, unlike those in the Light Way, were impossible to ignore. Lagan had asked for nothing more than to stay with him; Blor for a willingness to heal;

Raghna to trade muteness for speech.

Arturo had not demanded anything either until they had come south, and then only to remain with him until Bride's Day. She would soon have fulfilled her pledge but she was no longer intent on desertion. It was more efficient to kill Fada in a band than on her own.

They made their last camp in Cranoch Forest on the banks of a stream Caitlin called the Losch. Whatever its name, its sluggish flow dulled the Goddess's voice and tightened Etaine's nerves. While Cranoch Forest gifted them shelter, there were more pines than oaks, and Lisanisk's walls were visible away across an empty sweep of grass.

As dusk fell, news spread that the rest of the Rangers were to join them there *or at least those who had survived*, Etaine amended grimly. The prospect of reuniting with their comrades cheered the Rangers but Etaine remained tense knowing Cormac would broach the subject of coupling again before they entered Lisanisk.

The birdcalls gave way to the quiet of stars and the smell of roasting meat drifted through the trees. Cormac moved amongst his Rangers speaking with them quietly but in the Emerald Way, Etaine felt his tension rise.

He feared other of his bands had met the same fate as Fionn's and as the night drew on, the Rangers' anxiety grew too until it hung in the air like the fire smoke. Etaine knew fear was the price of caring, as was grief as Caitlin had learned, but even before Isbeil's death, Caitlin's friendliness had gifted Etaine a sense of belonging she had not felt since Boath.

It was not a feeling she welcomed. Worry about others impeded her murderous mission and she had already caught herself hoping Caitlin was amongst those who marched out of Lisanisk at Bride's Day's end.

The moon had risen when Cormac brought Beathan and Asgall to the fire Etaine shared with Bress and Caitlin, and he wasted no time in questioning Bress and Caitlin about Lisanisk's layout. They were the only Rangers in Cormac's band who had visited the settlement and they described it in detail as they ate.

'There are three springs,' said Caitlin, 'which is why it draws so many on Bride's Day.'

'It makes for a brisk trade,' added Bress. 'Metal-workers, wood-workers, cloth- merchants, purveyors of foods you have never heard off, let alone tasted.'

'Adam's folk will be keen there is no trouble then,' said Cormac. 'Whatever Fada plan won't be obvious, not like Craith.'

'But just as deadly, no doubt,' said Asgall, and glanced at Etaine.

'Where are the springs located?' she asked Bress.

'In the north, east, and west quarters,' he said.

'At least they are not together,' said Etaine.

'Why is that important?' asked Cormac sharply.

'Craith's springs were in the heart of Craith and so the feasting and dancing were there too. It made it easier for Fada to encircle us and once we were trapped in the Hall, easier for them to fight off those who tried to break in.'

Bress and Caitlin's shock reminded Etaine that most of the Rangers were unaware she had been at Craith, let alone been caught, and Caitlin's warm hand closed over hers. 'It won't be a tactic they can use this time around,' she said. 'The springs are well-spaced.'

'Where do the streams exit the walls?' asked Etaine.

'They do not,' said Bress.

'But that is not possible,' interjected Beathan.

'It is if they bubble up from underground rivers,' said Cormac.

Caitlin shrugged. 'I have not heard of underground

rivers although it makes sense. The springs' water is pure and sweet and never runs low. Their reliability and the trade they draw are all that Adam's folk care about.'

'How many Fada actually live in Lisanisk?' asked Cormac.

'I have not been there for a couple of years. The last time I visited, I am guessing there were close to a hundred. At least with no she-Fada, they are not seeding children.'

'Not here,' said Cormac. 'They keep their children safely elsewhere while they murder ours.' His voice held such bitterness that, for a while, the only sound was the crack of burning cones.

'A hundred seems about right,' said Bress eventually. 'Their temples hold about thirty and as they have only built three, I am guessing their numbers have not increased.'

'Adam's folk allow Fada temples?' gasped Etaine.

'Adam's folk allow most things that add to trade,' said Bress. 'Since the temples were built, taverns have sprung up nearby to accommodate Fada who come to worship. The springs remain accessible to true-Eadar, lesser-Eadar, Adam's folk and Fada so no group has any cause for complaint.' Bress smiled sourly. 'The words of Lisanisk's trader-leaders or *Maors* as they call themselves, not mine.

'They are happy to have Rangers in Lisanisk for the same reason, as long as there is no trouble. As far as the Maors are concerned, Fada and Eadar will smile and nod to each other in the streets and once we are beyond their walls, we are no longer their concern. At least that is what it was like a couple of years ago and I do not imagine it has changed.'

'So Lisanisk's Maors do not want another Craith because it will be bad for trade,' said Asgall sourly.

'Which confirms that whatever Fada intend, it is not a public slaughter,' said Cormac.

'A private one more likely,' said Etaine. 'Are there

caves in Lisanisk, Caitlin?'

'Not that I know of. Buildings press right up against the walls.'

'Why—' began Cormac but at that moment, movement through the trees heralded the arrival of Gil's band and Cormac rose to welcome them. Dermot's band arrived shortly afterwards, but it was close to midnight before Niall's band came in.

There was a palpable easing of tension when they appeared but as Etaine watched Cormac and Caitlin move off with Cian, she knew there were some this night whose hearts would be filled with grief rather than joy.

The bands ate together but their conversations did not last much longer than their meals and those not guarding soon took to their bedrolls. Etaine remained at the fire. She'd had trouble even choking down food and knew it would be pointless trying to sleep. Cormac sat with the other Ceannards and she guessed they discussed strategies.

They wasted their breath. The only way to defeat Fada was to kill them before they killed you. The Goddess's muffled voice added to Etaine's agitation and she set off upstream to search for a place where Her voice might be clearer, but it was hard to think of anything other than Fada.

She knew from Craith they believed the Serpent was vulnerable on Bride's Day because the Eadar's *foul* worship drew it closer to the surface. Sickening images of the slate-eyed Fada who had demanded she reveal its domain swarmed back and she lurched sideways into an oak and then sprang back and drew her knives.

But what stepped from the shadows was no Fada but a stag, its antlers as magnificent as the oak's spreading branches. It flung up its head, not in challenge but in triumph, and the darkness suffused with emerald light.

You survived! The Serpent is stronger than stone!

Etaine blinked and when the Light Way returned, the stag had gone. It had delivered a message or else the Emerald Way had, and one that echoed Cormac's demand to seed another child. Etaine shook her head in angry rebuttal. She would *not* risk another Ellair! She would fight and die in the Light Way and, despite what Cormac believed, the fight in Lisanisk might be just as public as Craith's. And all Fada had to do afterwards, was to wait until the Maor readmitted them to their settlements, and they *would* readmit them, because trade was more important to Adam's folk than Eadar lives.

A pale smudge floated on the stream's surface and Etaine started. It was the reflection of an owl perched on a pine on the opposite bank. She took a steadying breath then froze. It was *Raghna's* face that now shimmered on the water.

You must!

Etaine reeled as the words sounded in her head. The owl still stared at her from the pine and Etaine's gaze flashed back to the water, but it was empty as the owl took flight. Why had Raghna appeared to her in owl form? And then Etaine's mouth dried as she realised the crone had appeared in her *true* form. Her thoughts swung to the stag and she had no need of the Emerald Way to know it was Blor.

Etaine wandered on, so dazed that she scarcely knew where she went. Blor had healed her body; Raghna her mind; and Arturo had protected her since. But why serve the Fuaran? And Etaine was certain now it *was* the Fuaran who directed the shifters, one way or another. She cannot have been the only Eadar the Fuaran had rescued that terrible night either, so had the other survivors been guarded by shifters too? Or only her? And most troubling of all:

why had the Fuaran gone to so much trouble?

Etaine craved the Goddess's guidance but Her voice remained indistinct and she wondered whether the Losch fed one of Lisanisk's springs and if it did, whether loathsome Fada temples had sullied the Goddess's voice. Etaine did not know how She could bear the foul gods of the Fada so close or how *she* would bear being near Fada.

Once they were within Lisanisk's walls, the only thing she would have control over was whether she only risked herself or a child as well. Cian had been right to avoid seeding a child with Isbeil and yet Etaine could not ignore Blor and Raghna's appearance their true forms or their message.

She settled on the bank and stared at the water blankly. It was natural that a Toiseach would search for weapons to defeat Fada, she conceded, and Cormac had Remembered enough of the Serpent to sense its power. She wanted nothing more than to defeat Fada too, but Cormac had only been a Ranger when he had abandoned her and Ellair, and now he bore responsibilities many times greater than a Ceannard. A Toiseach must serve the needs of *all* his Rangers *and* Lisanisk's Eadar, not just his mate or child's. And even if they *did* seed another child, it might not be enough.

Etaine sensed the Serpent's power but she also sensed its subtlety. The Eadar's struggles might be as inconsequential to it as the Losch's pebbles or it might even resent the Eadar's intrusion and react violently. There were other risks too. Cormac might *know* he must stay with her and their child but not *feel* it and if he abandoned them a second time?

Lagan had saved her and Ellair in Boath but it had cost him his life, and while she could call on Donal or even Taig, she would not risk condemning them to the same fate, and that meant taking the child with her into death.

She groaned and cradled her head in her hands.

'Etaine?'

It was Cormac and she scrambled up, gripped by the wild idea he was about to transform into his namesake the raven. 'It is late,' he said. 'You should be sleeping.'

'So should you,' she snapped, rattled by the night's revelations.

'I have been in discussion with the Ceannards. It might be our last chance to meet as a group. It will certainly be more difficult to come together in Lisanisk.'

'Why?'

'We have decided to disperse throughout the settlement.'

'That will make it easier for them to pick us off.'

'Not if we stay in bands,' he said. 'After Craith, massing might be even more dangerous. Do you have a better strategy?'

'Burn the Fada temples to the ground with them inside.'

Cormac grunted. 'You know that is not possible. Have you thought further on my suggestion?'

'Yes.'

'And?'

'I won't risk another Craith.'

Cormac's eyes flashed as he stepped closer. 'Because you do not trust me? Because you think I will abandon you again? Or is the notion of coupling with me repellent?'

'You know the reason.'

'Do I? You are risking the lives of other Eadar children, the other *Ellairs* you have sworn to protect. Calling on the powers of the Emerald and Serpent Ways as true-Eadar once did could help us defeat Fada, but you refuse to even countenance the idea. I begin to wonder, Etaine, whether you are using Craith as an excuse; whether, in fact, you have come to love murdering more than mothering.'

He stormed off but Etaine was too incensed to follow. Part of her knew his harshness stemmed from tension over what lay ahead but knowing did nothing to quell her anger. Cormac had been so poorly connected to the Emerald Way he had not known he had seeded a child, let alone protected it and now he was an expert on the Emerald Way *and* on the Serpent Way as well!

There was a beech amongst the pines, its narrow trunk reminiscent of a Fada and Etaine flung her belt-knives at it, her sleeve-knives and in one smooth sweep, her boot-knives too. The throws were true and by chance, formed a star pattern on the trunk. She smiled grimly. Twelve knives for twelve Fada and all with the Goddess's star-blessing.

She reclaimed her knives, pulled out her sharp-stone and settling on the bank, honed each in turn. The task helped her shut out the Emerald Way where Cormac waited with none of the anger he had just shown. Twelve knives for twelve Fada, she repeated silently as she made her way back to camp. Given the loss of the Goddess's voice, she could at least take comfort in that.

22

They left Cranoch Forest at dawn and set off over the grasslands. Arturo had returned to her side but Etaine kept her gaze straight ahead. His recent absences made her feel as if he had already returned to the wilds and she sensed she would soon follow, not to where he roamed but to the Emerald Way, and afterwards, to wherever death led.

She watched the new sun edge the clouds with bright fire; breathed in the dewy scents of grass; and sifted the chaffinch's cry from the jay's. She wanted to imprint these things on her memory before she passed beyond Lisanisk's stone walls. There would only be time for fighting there and she sensed she would never walk these lands again.

Cormac had kept them in the same bands but had formed them up, Fada-style, to march into Lisanisk. Niall's band marched behind theirs followed by Gil and Dermot's. While Cormac knew the sight of sixty, armed and marching Eadar might alarm the Maors, he wanted to make it clear to Fada that Rangers would meet force with force.

He strode along at the head of the band while Asgall marched in front of her, Beathan behind, and Arturo and Caitlin to either side. Cormac's intention might have been to protect her, but it was more likely to ensure she obeyed his commands. Conversation rippled through the ranks and Etaine learned that Dermot's band was to guard the northern spring, Gil's the western, and Niall's the eastern. Their own band would aid Cormac's overall command and be deployed if necessary.

'Gil has got the best posting,' murmured Caitlin, as Lisanisk's walls drew ever closer. The Gate Guard were visible now and Etaine's hand rested on a belt-knife. 'Duath and Deas Nathairs are smaller and there are fewer taverns and trade there. Iar Nathair is where most of the trade, music, and dance will be. And Eadar, of course,' she added.

'That is what they call the springs?'

'Yes. The Unremembered names for north, east, and west springs. These lands were special to the Fuaran long before Adam's folk built Lisanisk.'

Caitlin was correct about *duath*, *deas* and *iar* being the Fuaran words for north, east, and west but the Fuaran word for spring was *fuaran*, from which they took their own name in honour of the Goddess; *nathair* actually meant snake or *serpent*. An emerald mist pulsed about her and she sensed Cormac's stride falter as the compulsion to complete their link strengthened, but she clenched her teeth and focussed on the Light Way.

And then they heard horses, coming fast, from behind. Fear surged through the Rangers and some even broke ranks before Cormac's command brought them back into line. Fada would not attack within sight of the wall but word passed down the ranks to prepare. Hands rested on knife hafts and sword hilts, and bows were slipped from shoulders. Etaine drew two belt knives, glanced back, and counted quickly. Sixteen horses; four riderless.

They *had* to be the Fada who had murdered Fionn's band and given the riderless horses, Fionn's band had sent four of them into death. Etaine tightened her grip on her knives and calculated the speed of their approach. If they passed to the right she would have a brief window to throw before Caitlin and those in front blocked her aim. The same to the left, where Arturo walked.

She was aware that Cormac's attention had sharpened on her in the Emerald Way, but she concentrated on the horses. They did not slow and Etaine feared the Rangers were to be run down but at the last moment the Fada split and thundered past on either side. The manoeuvre was intended to intimidate *and* mock and Fada mouths bent in smiles as they passed.

Adam's folk interpreted their smiles as friendliness but the Eadar saw them for what they were: the barred teeth of creatures on the attack. Fada had taunted Eadar in Craith too but Etaine was familiar with their tricks and kept her focus on the speed of their horses. She would take down the final riders, on the left first with her favoured throwing hand, and by the time the lead riders brought their mounts around, the Rangers would be in defensive positions and have loosed a storm of arrows.

The last of the horses galloped past and Etaine's left arm flicked back with lightning speed, but Beathan caught her wrist in a crushing grip. 'You know the Toiseach's orders,' he growled.

Etaine tried to break free and was jostled from behind by the next rank of Rangers, and Beathan did not release her until Fada were out of range, then he shoved her roughly back into line. If he had hit her on the back, rather than on shoulder, she would have crumpled to the ground but even so, pain speared through her. The Emerald Way beckoned with its promise of respite, but Cormac waited there with his anger at her disobedience and she kept marching.

'Are you alright?' asked Caitlin, touching her arm.

Etaine nodded, not trusting herself to speak. Three

more days, she reiterated silently. Then she would be quit of the likes of Cormac and Beathan and free to kill as many Fada as she liked.

Cormac brought them to a halt at the gate and they remained in formation while a Maor offered the traditional words of welcome and wish for a fair Bride's Day. He had the solid build and reddish-brown hair typical of Adam's folk and while he was polite, his warnings about not disturbing the peace and threats of expulsion took a lot longer to deliver than his welcome.

The Maor wore the bright colours Adam's folk favoured and so did the Guard, but the Maor had gold trim on their jackets to show their status. A second Maor laboriously recorded the Ceannard's names and Ranger numbers in ink while the band waited.

'Do they not trust their memories?' muttered Etaine.

'My kin say it comes from their life of trade,' whispered Caitlin. 'So much passes through their settlements even true-Eadar would have trouble remembering it.'

The Guard finally waved them through and they marched into Lisanisk. Fada lounged in the wall's shadow and Etaine felt their hateful gazes on her. Their regard had always repulsed her but there was something particularly malevolent in the mix and she turned. A Fada smiled at her, his eyes as blank as slate, and in an instant Lisanisk was sucked into a darkness filled Ellair's screams and burning flesh.

Caitlin's warm hand caught and squeezed hers and Etaine somehow managed to keep walking. 'He was at Craith,' she said hoarsely.

'I guessed so. Tell Cormac the vile filth recognised you. Fada are vindictive; he will seek to injure you further.'

The owl remained motionless in the pine at the forest's edge and the Fuaran waited too until the gates closed behind the Rangers. The stag had gone, far from the place of arrows and spears, yet fear of the hunter was but a small part of the dread that haunted the lands. It seeped through the earth and resonated in the deeper ways of water and cave, and it rose with the tree-sap to hang in the air like a malevolent mist. It tormented the Goddess's springs and streams and rivers too and clouded Her clear voice.

The owl came to ground and rocked from foot to foot. 'The place of stone and broken trees is perilous for Arturo,' it said.

'All Ways are perilous now,' said the Fuaran. 'I must prepare.'

The owl beat its wings. 'I will wait for him.'

'He will come soon or not at all.'

'I will wait,' the owl repeated, calm now and determined.

The Fuaran nodded. 'Everything waits—but not forever.'

23

Etaine found the march through Lisanisk almost pleas-ant compared to the Fada-infested gate. Lesser-Eadar and Adam's folk crowded the streets and as Cormac led the Rangers up between the buildings, lesser-Eadar bowed and touched their brows. Adam's folk simply stared; the she- at the he-Eadar, the he- at Etaine and Caitlin, and the children at them all.

The Rangers' beaded-braids flashed clear, gold, and green in their long hair and while the attention of Adam's folk was drawn by the sight of so many emerald-eyed, white-skinned, black-haired Eadar in one place, the Rang-ers' attention was drawn by the traders' stalls.

Bronze and copper trinkets sparkled in the sun and there were the brittle honey treats Etaine remembered from Boath and Craith. Judging by what else was on of-fer, Lisanisk was both a bigger *and* wealthier settlement. There were gold and silver pressed into bowls and cups and beautifully engraved; anklets and bracelets and rings and necklaces of bronze and silver set with gems; bolts of glittering fabric; and ribbons that fluttered in the breeze, their crimson, blue, and yellow colours shocking after the greens and browns of the journey.

Music added to the crowd's noise; players of harps and pipes on every corner, begging coin as revellers passed by. The streets were not devoid of Fada either; their height, grey clothing and sombreness making them stand out, and Etaine's grip tightened on a belt-knife.

Dermot, Gil, and Niall's bands peeled off in the directions of the springs they were to guard and Cormac led the remaining Rangers deeper into Lisanisk. It was almost dusk before he secured lodgings because Lisanisk turned out to be unusually crowded even for Bride's Day.

According to the tavern-keeper who accepted Cormac's coin, the springs at Ardaroch, Scarrnaen and Odhar had dropped away and many who would have celebrated Bride's Day there had come to Lisanisk instead to thank the Goddess. Lisanisk's springs remained pure and bountiful, the tavern-keeper boasted. The news added to Etaine's disquiet. If Fada had interfered with the springs to drive more Eadar into Lisanisk, it suggested an attack every bit as deadly as Craith.

Their lodgings were behind the tavern, which was already full, and reached by a narrow laneway. The building was long and low and had regularly spaced doorways that opened out onto the yard at the tavern's back. To Etaine it looked like the buildings in Craith where Fada housed their horses. Being single-storeyed made it vulnerable to attack but easier to escape from than the tavern, which had rooms reached by narrow staircases and windows with sheer drops to the yard below.

Etaine guessed the tavern's rooms were more richly furnished than the one she and Caitlin were allocated but even it was luxurious compared to a bedroll on the ground. There were two straw-mattressed beds and washstands with pitchers of water set ready for drinking and washing and, while it was chill inside, there was plenty of wood stacked on the hearth.

She washed off the journey's grime and perched on the bed while Caitlin bathed, brushed out her long hair and adjusted her braid-beads. Etaine had once been just as proud of her hair, which had fallen below her waist, but at some point in the weeks of delirium that followed her branding, Blor had shaved it off.

There had not seemed much point in regrowing it or on wasting time with braid-beads, given Fada would soon end her life. Caitlin half turned as she reached for her shirt and Etaine stiffened. The she-Eadar was slender but her breasts were full, and her belly rounded. 'You carry,' gasped Etaine.

'Yes,' said Caitlin, busy with her buttons.

Etaine sprang from her perch and went to her. 'But the father must be with you! Is he of Cormac's band? We must bring him here at once or you must go to him!'

'Do not fret, Etaine. I carry more Adam's blood than you and he does too. We do not face the coupling demands of true-Eadar. He is close enough and I am content.'

'I do not understand why you would seed a child now,' muttered Etaine, pacing in agitation.

'If we waited for a time free of Fada threat, there would be no Eadar children at all,' said Caitlin, pulling on her jacket. 'And, despite what might happen in the next few days, I am glad to carry. Isbeil would not take the risk and now it is too late for her but I have still got the chance to go home with my mate after Lisanisk and raise our child.'

The fact that Caitlin carried explained how she knew of the time difference in the Emerald Way, realised Etaine, *and* of a he-Eadar's responsibilities to his mate and, while Caitlin had journeyed without difficulty, carrying put her at terrible risk. Fada in Craith had taken delight in murdering carrying she-Eadar and boasted how they prevented the Eadar's demonic spawn from drawing breath.

Despite Caitlin's reassurances, Etaine kept close to her as they made their way to the tavern to eat. The tavern-keeper had set lamps, but the throw of light was poor and the yard's corners remained in darkness.

Their lodgings might have been sparsely furnished but the food the tavern-keeper provided gave no cause for complaint. Servers delivered dishes of roast hare and mashed turnips doused in rich gravy, and plates piled high with fresh oaten-bread. Etaine had not eaten turnips since Craith and after years of foraged greens, they were heavy and sweet.

Most of the band were already there and she and Caitlin settled at a table with Arturo and Bress. Artair and Tormod soon joined them but Etaine barely listened to their conversation; distracted by Caitlin's willingness to risk a child. Caitlin's views on the subject echoed Cormac's and she watched him as he moved from table to table in speech with his Rangers. The she- in the room watched him too and Etaine knew why.

The beads in his long black hair caught the lamplight and his white skin and dark emerald eyes made him everything a he-Eadar should be. The pulse of yearning that had engulfed her seven years ago in Boath intensified and, as their unfinished link burned as bright as fire, she wrenched her gaze back to her plate.

If she had not allowed him to kiss her, their link might have remained unguessed at and she just another of his Rangers. But the link had made her hungry for his touch. She sensed him settle opposite but kept her eyes on her meal as if hare and turnip were the most fascinating things in the world.

'We start early on the morrow,' he said, keeping his voice low, for lesser-Eadar and Adam's folk ate nearby.

'The bands will reconnoitre the springs and the Ceannards report to me by midday. I do not want any Rangers on their own. Tormod, Artair, and Bress; you are with me. Etaine, Caitlin, and Arturo; I want you at Iar Nathair. It will be obvious Gil's band guards there but I want you to wander about as if simply enjoying Bride's Day Eve. Look for *anything* that seems out of place.'

'Yes, Toiseach,' said Caitlin.

'Etaine, I gave explicit orders *not* to attack Fada at Lisanisk and yet you would have had Beathan not prevented it. Have you an explanation?' The Rangers at the table continued to eat but the air had brittled.

'We were beyond the wall,' she said, her gaze on a point over his shoulder.

'But within *clear* sight of the Maor *and* Guard.' He dropped his voice lower, but it resonated with anger. 'I *won't* risk us being expelled from Lisanisk and leaving the Eadar here unprotected because *you* are too *ill-disciplined* to control yourself. If you *breach* my orders again, *you* will spend the *rest* of Bride's Day's celebrations in the *cells* Maor reserve for those who drink too much mead. Is that understood?'

'Yes, Toiseach.'

'And you felt something as we passed the gate. What was it?'

'One of the Fada there was at Craith.'

'He recognised you?'

'Yes, Toiseach.'

Cormac's expression remained unchanged but she felt the ructions in the Emerald Way. 'If the Fada recognised you, he knows we have first-hand knowledge of their tactics in Craith and are prepared for similar here,' he said. '*If* they intended to repeat the same style of attack, I doubt they will now, given our numbers. But the question remains as to what they *do* intend.'

No one spoke and Cormac placed some coins on the table. 'You will look less suspicious tomorrow if you trade for the treats and trinkets on offer. And,' he added more lightly, 'Bride's Day festivities always provide something pretty to catch a she-Eadar's eye.' Caitlin swooped on the coins and Arturo took his share but Etaine left hers untouched, and Cormac's gaze settled on her. 'Nothing here to tempt the beautiful Etaine?'

'Nothing, Toiseach.'

'Then more for Caitlin and Arturo,' he said briskly. 'You will report to me tomorrow noon,' he said, and moved away.

The tavern was warm and it was not long before Caitlin was yawning. She rose and bade the rest of the table Fair Dreams and Etaine rose too, hastened after her out of the tavern, and stepped in front to scan the yard. Noise spilled from the street as Adam's folk traded in preparation for their festival feasts and Etaine struggled to separate sounds of normalcy from those of threat. The shadowed yard added to her tension as did the trees' overhang at its far end.

'The Toiseach has set guards,' said Caitlin, shivering behind her and when Etaine did not move, nudged her. 'Come, it is cold.'

Etaine continued to scan as she followed Caitlin to their lodgings and she barred the door as soon as they were inside. Servers had lit the lamps but not the fire and the room was chill.

'I will set the fire,' said Etaine. 'You get some rest.'

Caitlin pulled off her boots and slid under the blankets but propped on her elbow and watched Etaine. 'You puzzle me,' she said after a little. 'I can sense your link with the Toiseach in the Emerald Way, in fact, it is so strong even uncoupled Rangers can sense it but in the Light Way …'

She shrugged. 'They say you were mate-paired in Boath seven years ago but you left with another Ranger. Is that true?'

'Yes.'

'Why?'

Etaine sat back on her haunches, her gaze on the new flame. 'I thought the Toiseach was my true-mate. I was wrong.'

'So, the Ranger you left with was your true-mate?'

'No.'

'So, you have been wrong twice?'

'I have been wrong many times, Caitlin,' said Etaine dryly.

'It is obvious to everyone the Toiseach wants you back.'

Etaine came and settled on the edge of her bed. 'The Toiseach wants a weapon to use against Fada. He thinks I can provide it.'

'The Serpent?' whispered Caitlin, and Etaine nodded. 'We might be in the right place,' said Caitlin, and glanced about nervously. 'There are tales told in the surrounding cots that go back to ancient times, beyond even the times Unremembered,' she continued softly. 'They say of all the Eadar lands, it is here in Lisanisk, where the Serpent dwells closest to the Light Way. They say the Fuaran set great stones amongst the oaks to mark where She might rise but the stones were lost when Adam's folk cleared the forest. The Fuaran were lost too but many believe the Serpent remains.'

Etaine made no response, simply pulled off her jacket and boots and slipped under the covers. She kept her sleeve- and belt-knives in place because if Caitlin had heard such tales, Fada would have too. It all but guaranteed they would make another attempt to destroy the Serpent and, having learned from their failure at Craith, they would be more likely to succeed.

24

They left their lodgings a little after sunrise but being Bride's Day Eve, the streets were already busy, and it took them a long time to reach the western quarter. At least their slow pace gave Caitlin time to describe Lisanisk's layout. Etaine learned the Fuaran had worn tracks between the springs and that they had not approached the springs directly but circled them in ever narrowing spirals.

Adam's folk had found the practice curious and time-consuming but as the Fuaran's trackways were etched into the earth, it had been easier to pave them than lay out new ones, which was why Lisanisk's three main trackways were circuitous.

It seemed obvious to Etaine the Fuaran had created a giant triskele in honour of the triple Goddess but she held her tongue. Caitlin carried a child, but she was not true-Eadar and Etaine had no idea how much Caitlin Remembered of the Serpent. Nor did she want to increase Caitlin's peril by adding to her knowledge, given Fada's vile presence.

Adam's folk had named the Fuaran's trackways the Duath, Deas and Iar Ways after the springs they serviced but, as Lisanisk had grown, a tangle of connecting streets had cut across them. Even so, they remained the quickest routes through Lisanisk *and* to the walls, for Adam's folk had extended the trackways beyond the springs right up to the wall gates.

Etaine considered how long it would take to sprint from Iar Nathair to the gates and whether the Guard would bar them, and if they *did* escape the walls, whether mounted Fada could run them down before they reached the trees.

More stalls appeared as they drew closer to Iar Nathair, so that they lined both sides of the street, and added to the crush. Chimes hung from their canopies to tinkle in the breeze, along with beribboned sticks, and glittering scarves. Etaine stared at the traders' wares as she passed.

Some offered poorly crafted images of bats or bears, made from metals more tin than silver, but others had beautiful pendants of the Goddess in her fiery and watery forms, and as the triskele: the Goddess uncoupled, coupled, and crone. These were worked in gleaming silver and Etaine briefly wished she had taken Cormac's coin. There were Bride's crosses too, delicately woven in silver wire with small creatures set in their centres. These were favoured by children and Etaine had traded for them for Ellair.

She would have hastened past but Caitlin stopped to haggle over a cross set with a squirrel. Etaine waited next to her and Arturo moved to the next stall for the way was narrow. He stood stolidly, his gaze on those who passed, but Etaine knew in spirit he was in some rushing stream, his great paws trawling for fish, or in a stormy night, his snout raised to the tumult while the Goddess's sweet water drenched his pelt.

Caitlin finished the trade but as they re-joined the throng, something struck Etaine in the back and the world

171

exploded in pain. She felt herself falling and only Caitlin's fast reflexes stopped her hitting the paving.

'Who was it?' growled Arturo, suddenly beside her, but Etaine could scarcely breathe let alone speak. It was akin to being branded a second time.

'Fada,' spat Caitlin. 'The same filth as at the gate. Have they stabbed you?'

Etaine still could not speak but she sensed Arturo's movement in the Fada's direction and caught his arm. She guessed Fada had slammed her in the back with something blunt like a knife haft but nothing good could come of a brawl in the street, especially since no wound had been inflicted.

'You aren't bleeding,' said Caitlin in confusion. She and Arturo were holding her upright between them and Etaine heard the impatient grunts of those who struggled to pass. So did Caitlin. 'There are seats on the edge of the square, Arturo. I will sit her there. If you could get some mead, it might help.' Caitlin helped her on but Etaine still could not straighten and she only knew the crowd had thinned when fewer feet crossed her line of vision.

Caitlin finally eased her down onto a stone seat. 'You are in so much pain,' she muttered, 'but there is no blood. Let me see.' And before Etaine could stop her, she slid her hand up under Etaine's shirt.

'Sweet Goddess!' she gasped. 'Sweet, sweet Goddess.' Caitlin's breathing was as ragged as Etaine's and Etaine caught her hand and held it tight. She still could not speak but the pain had dulled from boiling metal to boiling water. She sensed Arturo's return, felt him guide a mug to her lips and gulped down mead. It made her cough but its heady sweetness allowed her to straighten.

'The band knew you had been at Craith,' muttered Caitlin, 'but no one knew you had ...' she took a shuddering breath. 'Does Cormac know?' Etaine nodded. 'I am surprised he is not out murdering every Fada in Lisanisk with his bare hands!'

'Cormac is Toiseach,' Etaine managed to say. 'His care is for all the Eadar.'

'Maybe,' said Caitlin. 'But his love is for you.'

Silence stretched and the pain eased enough for Etaine to take in her surroundings. She was seated on the edge of a large, paved square and directly in front was a stone building with a flat stone roof. It was at odds with the age-silvered shingled roofs of the surrounding houses and the building's walls jarred too. They were made of pillars with gaps between them and as Etaine watched, she became aware that Eadar and Adam's folk passed in and out.

'What is that?' she asked.

'A Fada temple. The spring's underneath.'

'Fada have built their temple *over* the spring?' gasped Etaine.

'Yes. Subtle, aren't they?'

'But that means . . .' Etaine stumbled to a stop as fury added to her pain.

'That their foul gods crouch over the Goddess and that those who seek the Goddess's blessings or offer Her thanks, must do so under the hateful gazes of their stone gods.'

'But why do Adam's folk allow it?' demanded Etaine. 'They rule Lisanisk, do they not?'

'Adam's folk see no problem in different gods living side by side and, of course, as their gods live in the clouds, it does not affect them.'

Etaine was too incensed to say more, just sipped the mead as she watched the spring's visitors cross the square. Those who looked to be more Adam's blood did not seem to mind entering a Fada temple to honour the Goddess, but truer Eadar looked grim as they made their way across the paving.

Two older she-Eadar went past, arm in arm, and dis-appeared inside and then a mother and an older she-child of Adam's blood, followed by a coupled he- and she-Eadar with their child. The he-child danced about them waving a beribboned stick. All three had the black hair, white skin, and emerald eyes of true-Eadar and the child looked the age Ellair would have been had he lived.

'See anything unusual?' asked Caitlin after a while.

'Only a grotesque Fada building,' muttered Etaine.

'What about you, Arturo?' asked Caitlin.

'Not many Fada,' said Arturo briefly.

Etaine scanned the square. He was right. 'Not like Craith,' she said. 'The streets were crawling with them but I have no doubt their intentions are even deadlier here.'

'I wish we knew what they were,' said Caitlin in frus-tration. 'I might take a stroll around the square.'

'The Toiseach said to stay together,' said Arturo.

'Gil's band is about and I will keep in vision range,' said Caitlin and set off.

Arturo obeyed Cormac's commands but he was not given to reminding others of them and Etaine wondered if he sensed something amiss. She certainly did. The square reeked of malevolence, as if the very earth itself felt the Fada's murderous intent.

Etaine gripped the edge of the seat as she watched Caitlin's progress, the browns and blacks of her Ranger clothes easy to pick amongst the colours of those who cel-ebrated Bride's Day Eve. Caitlin passed a group of Fada and Etaine's hand went to her knife as their heads turned, but they made no move to accost her.

Caitlin continued on and disappeared from view around the back of the temple. Time dragged and when she failed to emerge, Arturo rose and Etaine struggled upright too, but then she re-appeared and sauntered back.

'The Fada I passed included the one that hit you in

the back, the one you said had been at Craith. It is a pity the Toiseach ordered us only to watch. I was close enough to empty his guts on the stones. Do you know what the Toiseach plans?'

'No.'

'Maybe he will tell us when we get back. It is almost noon and the wind has chilled.' Caitlin pulled her jacket closer. 'I do not think Bride's Day is going to be pleasant if today is any guide. The crowds are already thinning.'

Caitlin was right; the cloud was building and those in the square quickened their steps towards the taverns, as did those who emerged from temple. The mother and grown she-child hurried past along with others of Adam's blood, but not the older she-Eadar or the couple with the he-child and Etaine watched the temple door anxiously. Those who emerged were either Adam's folk or carried so little Eadar blood as to be counted as such.

'Does the temple have a second entrance?' she asked Caitlin, keeping her eyes on it.

'Only the one at the front. Why?'

'Did you notice a true-Eadar couple come out? They had a he-child with them with a ribboned-stick.'

'No,' said Caitlin, and inhaled sharply. 'You aren't suggesting Fada are murdering Eadar *inside* the temple, are you?'

'Yes.'

'But where would they hide the bodies?'

'In the spring.'

'But they would be missed.'

'Not immediately. The tavern-keeper said Lisanisk is so busy because the surrounding springs had sunk and Eadar have come here. They would not be missed for days and even when their kin came looking, they would find nothing.'

'By the Goddess,' choked Caitlin. 'I hope you are

wrong.'

So did Etaine but the idea of murdering Eadar *inside* the temple held a terrible logic. The Fada's victims would conveniently come to them and there would be no corpses to upset the Maor.

Their return journey to the tavern was a lot swifter thanks to the weather which had emptied the streets. The traders had rolled down their canopies too. The Maor would not be pleased by the loss of coin, concluded Etaine sourly, as they hurried along. Caitlin kept pace beside her but Arturo dropped back, probably to prevent a second attack.

Another attack was unlikely though; the slate-eyed Fada had done what any coward could have but she had been a fool to give him the opportunity. She had been distracted and it was not a mistake she would make again.

'The ground is unhappy,' said Arturo behind her.

Etaine nodded. She had felt it at the square and sensed it stemmed from the imposition of the Fada temple over the spring. It was not surprising Arturo felt it too, given his shifter sensibilities, but that he voiced his concerns showed just how troubled he was.

And if the springs *were* awash with murdered Eadar, the Goddess would be troubled too. As for the Serpent; she did not know.

25

Lisanisk's leaden skies and biting wind did nothing to alleviate Etaine's anxiety but at least they reached their lodgings before the rain started. It poured down and then thunder and lightning joined the mix. Midday came and went accompanied by rain beating against the shutters but there was no sign of Cormac and Etaine worried his absence was due to Fada attack rather than weather. Caitlin had curled up on the bed but Etaine prowled around the room and it was mid-afternoon and Caitlin sleeping, before there was a knock at the door.

Etaine opened it cautiously, belt-knife in hand, but it was Asgall, heavily caped and with a message the Toiseach remained with Niall and Dermot and would hear their report later in the tavern. And as they were not rostered to guard, the Toiseach ordered they remain in their lodgings.

Asgall had disappeared back into the gloom before Etaine thought to ask why Cormac had cancelled their noon meeting and as she re-barred the door, she wondered whether he had reached the same conclusion as her about the temples. The weather would keep the Eadar indoors tonight but they would visit the springs on Bride's Day regardless of the cold and wet, as would many of Adam's folk.

The Eadar knew the importance of thanking the Goddess but Adam's folk were also keen for Her blessing, knowing if the springs failed, so too would their animals. Etaine continued to pace but was careful not to disturb Caitlin; remembering just how tired she had been early in her months of carrying.

It was dark before they made their way across the yard to the tavern. The rain had given way to a still night, but cloud remained, and the air was chill. 'I think it is going to snow,' said Caitlin, as she pulled up her hood. 'Lisanisk is known for its sudden icy blasts.'

Compared to the night outside, Etaine found the tavern over bright, over warm, and over-crowded. Arturo followed them in and she knew it was worse for him but his stolid face betrayed nothing. As usual, Caitlin seemed unaffected as she cheerfully followed the tavern-keeper to an empty table and it was not long before he returned with a jug of mead and three mugs.

'Let us hope the weather improves for Bride's Day,' he said, as he set them down. 'It has been an odd season so far. We have had rain when there should be none and then a lack. Now it seems the Goddess will send us snow.'

Or Fada's vile gods would, thought Etaine irritably. All she wanted was for Cormac to appear so they could go and clean Fada filth from their temples before they murdered even more Eadar.

A young server brought bowls of stew and fresh-baked bread, his red hair incongruous given his emerald eyes. 'The tavern is honoured to have Rangers as our guests,' he said softly, as he set the food down. 'Our more usual guests are Fada.'

He disappeared back into the kitchens but his words seemed like a warning and Etaine's hand slid to a belt-knife. Caitlin and Arturo seemed oblivious and wasted no time tucking into the stew and Etaine followed suit. She must be strong for the fighting that would inevitably come later that night and need a clear head too. She pushed the mug of mead away.

The night wore on with no sign of Cormac and Etaine's frustration gave way to a fear he and the rest of the band were already dead. Caitlin's suggestion that they probably toasted the Goddess in some other snug tavern did not help and she was considering going in search of them when they appeared.

Twelve heavily armed and grim-looking Eadar Rangers dinted the tavern's conversations, but they picked up again once the Rangers had settled at the tables. Cormac, Beathan, Asgall and Bress joined Etaine's table and the rest sat nearby. The red-haired server appeared again, this time helped by an older server who looked all Adam's blood, and the band's conversation focussed on the weather until the food and mead had been delivered.

'Dermot and Niall's bands report nothing amiss at their springs,' said Cormac, keeping his voice low as he broke the bread, 'and Gil's in agreement. We have carried out a thorough reconnoitre of the streets too. Things seem quiet.'

'They might *seem* quiet but they are not,' retorted Etaine, and recounted what she had seen at the temple.

'Are you certain they did not use another exit?' asked Cormac.

'There *are* no other exits.'

'Did you check?'

'I checked,' said Caitlin. 'I walked all the way around. There is another stone building inside the temple's pillars that encloses the spring. It has small, high-set windows but only a single door.'

Cormac's dark emerald eyes swung back to Etaine. 'My orders were for you to stay together. Where were you and Arturo?'

'We stayed at the edge of the square,' said Etaine. 'I could see Caitlin at all times.'

'Not if she went *around* the temple. Why did you separate?'

'It was my fault, Toiseach,' said Caitlin. 'Arturo reminded me of your orders but I wanted to stretch my legs. Etaine had to sit for a time after the Fada from Craith attacked her.'

Etaine felt the reverberation in the Emerald Way but the flash of Cormac's hand to his knife was obvious to all. 'Tell me!'

'We stopped at some stalls trading animal charms and Bride's Crosses and the like,' said Etaine reluctantly. 'Caitlin was …' She sensed Caitlin stiffen and half shrugged. 'You know what she-Eadar are like, Toiseach. We have not seen any baubles months. I made the mistake of being distracted and the Fada from Craith took advantage. He hit me in the back, probably with a knife haft, so not to leave any obvious wound.'

'That Fada is a danger to you, Etaine. He . . .'

'The Fada are a danger to us *all*! And while we sit here in comfort, they murder more Eadar! We need to scour them from their foul temples! Now! This night!'

'And where are the bodies of these murdered Eadar?'

'In the spring!'

'And the proof? Use your head, Etaine. The Maors' warning was clear: cause a disturbance and the Rangers will be expelled. And once we are beyond the walls, the Eadar will have no protection at all.'

'They have *no* protection now!' said Etaine furiously.

'Well, we both know how that can be remedied,' said Cormac.

There was a strained silence and Caitlin yawned noisily. 'With your permission, Toiseach, I will go to my bed.'

Cormac nodded, and Caitlin touched Etaine briefly on the shoulder as she passed. 'I will wish you Fair Dreams now, Etaine. I am sure to be asleep before you come in.'

Many of the band nodded their goodnights soon after, including Beathan and Asgall. Arturo went with them but Etaine doubted he went to his bed despite having little chance of the solace he sought within Lisanisk's walls.

Cormac summoned one of the servers to ask for water, but it took some time to arrive and they sat in silence until the jug was delivered. 'You have formed a friendship with Caitlin, I see,' he said, as he filled their mugs. 'I hoped you might when I quartered you together.'

'So I will become a nicely obedient she-Eadar like she is?' sneered Etaine.

'No, because it is not easy being a she-Eadar in an all he-Eadar band. Caitlin and Isbeil grew close because of it and since Isbeil's death, Caitlin needs she-Eadar company more than ever. I hoped the friendship would benefit you too.'

'Oh really? You forget I have Arturo.'

'No one *has* a shifter, Etaine.' The truth of Cormac's words stung and she clenched her jaw. 'Do not mistake me,' he continued on more gently. 'I have no doubt he helped you in the north in all sorts of ways and that he has protected you since. But Arturo is of the wilds; he cannot give you what you most need.'

'Oh, and I suppose you can?'

'I have more chance than Arturo.'

Etaine thrust back her chair and stood. 'I have been with Arturo three years, Toiseach. In the first, I could speak no more than a handful of words. In the second, Arturo carted every piece of burning wood and killed every creature we ate. In the third, he still had to hold me when my dreams were so evil I yearned to throw myself from the flet. And even when I was at my angriest, when I screamed

181

at the night and cursed the day, or when I was silent and refused the food he cooked, *he never abandoned me*!'

26

Etaine stormed out of the tavern and came to a stop in the yard to let her temper cool. The lamps had blown out and it was pitch black. The Rangers' quarters were in darkness too, which meant those who had left the tavern earlier already slept. She thought of Caitlin, snug in her bed, and of the child she carried, and shivered as she thought of the risk to them both. At least the street was quiet which, given the cold and the night's lateness, was scarcely surprising.

Their rooms were the second from the end and she paused with her hand on the door as she realised she would need to wake Caitlin to let her in, but the door was unbarred. The first thing she noticed was that, despite the fire, it was cold inside, and the second was that Caitlin's bed was empty. The hair stirred on the back of her neck. There was no sign of disturbance but she dismissed the idea Caitlin had gone to the latrines; every sense told her Fada had been there.

She hastened back across the yard and reached the tavern just as Cormac came out. 'Fada have Caitlin,' she exclaimed. 'We have to go after her.'

'Guards are set. Have you checked the latrines?'

'They have her!'

Cormac hailed the guards: Ringean and Raild from one end of the yard, and Tormod and Artair from the other. 'Anything to report?' he asked.

'Nothing, Toiseach.'

'Return to your posts.'

The Rangers retreated and Cormac pushed open the door to their room and held the lamp high. 'The ceiling,' hissed Etaine.

What she had not noticed in the light and had missed in the dark was a trap door that now swung open. 'It must connect the roof spaces,' she said. 'The red-haired server said Fada had used these quarters; they would know where to hide. We have to go!'

But Cormac did not shout for his Rangers; he went to Asgall and Beathan's room and Etaine followed. The three stood in conversation too low for Etaine to hear and she prowled up and down outside until Cormac ordered her in. 'You will freeze,' he said, 'and the last thing I need is a sick she-Eadar.'

Beathan and Asgall had donned their jackets but Cormac appeared in no hurry to leave. 'Why would Fada risk coming here to take only Caitlin?' he demanded of her. 'You would think they would drop into other rooms and kill Rangers as they slept and yet they seem content only to carry one of us away.'

'They took her because they could! We need to go!

'Rushing down there is exactly what they intend and I am not about to offer up more Eadar lives. And if they *do* have Caitlin, I am guessing there is more to her taking than luring us into their foul temple, is there not, Etaine?'

Asgall and Beathan's regard was intense but she kept her attention on Cormac. 'They saw us together at Iar Na-thair,' she said hurriedly. 'They know we are friends and want to hurt me by hurting her. I escaped them at Craith and Fada do not tolerate being thwarted. The Fada who branded me knows I will come after her.'

'Is there another reason they would take her?'

'Is not wanting to kill me enough?'

Cormac's eyes bored into hers and Etaine had trouble meeting his gaze. Caitlin had not given Etaine permission to reveal she carried and, as the child's father was in Cormac's band, Cormac might be angered by the deceit. Fada would not know Caitlin carried anyway *except* they had seen her trade for the children's Bride's Cross! Etaine's heart pounded and she swallowed dryly.

'Fada won't have the opportunity to kill you because you will remain here, under increased guard,' snapped Cormac. 'The three of us will reconnoitre—quietly.'

'Reconnoitre? What use will that be? You will see nothing from the outside! And if I do not show up, they *will* kill her! I am not about to let that happen, Toiseach!'

'If you go racing down there, they will kill you *and* her! And we both know how they will do it. Her first, in front of you, and then you slowly to wring out every last moment of pain. You will stay here.'

'I will not!'

'That is an order!'

Etaine wrenched the signe from her neck and threw it at his feet. 'You have got what you always wanted, Toiseach. I am out of your band and out of your life!' And with that she turned and fled into the night.

Etaine's blood was up but her swift journey through the streets was far from reckless. She used dense pools of shadow to mask her progress, not that it was necessary; given it was past midnight, the streets were all but deserted. It would be different as the light grew; lovers favoured the first light of Bride's Day to seek the Goddess's blessing.

Flakes of snow drifted down, silver against the darkness and, as she ran, Etaine was gripped by a strange sense of exhilaration, as if an over-arching pattern to her life had been revealed.

Seven years ago, on this day, she had joined with Cormac and seeded Ellair and, on the same day, Cormac had abandoned them. Five years later, on this day, Fada had branded her and murdered their child and, on this Bride's Day, she had finally freed herself from Cormac's power over her as a Ranger, and over her heart as a false-mate. It was fitting her life would end on Bride's Day too, *and* at the Goddess's spring. She just hoped that, in the chaos, Caitlin and the precious life *she* carried, might somehow escape.

Etaine knew there was no point in devising a strategy. She fought best when she opened herself to the Emerald Way and let the Goddess guide her, but even with the Goddess's help, she would be unable to defeat the many Fada who lay in wait.

Her recklessness might grant her a small but temporary advantage, for Fada did not sacrifice themselves even for their gods and she had seen them abandon their friends in fights and run.

The slate-eyed Fada who had goaded her in Craith and driven the knife haft into the old wound since would seek to maximise her terror and helplessness. She guessed he would remind her of Ellair's death and emphasise she was to lose her she-Eadar friend as well. He would crow about Fada power and their gods' rule of the rise and ripple of the Goddess's spring; of how Eadar corpses polluted the very Goddess they professed to love.

She had twelve knives and must use them all, killing faster than at any time before. It would be a good way to end the time loaned to her since Craith. And then, if the

Goddess still smiled on her, perhaps in the Emerald Way or even in the Serpent Way, she would find Ellair, know him in spirit, and never be parted from him again.

Etaine did not stop at the edge of the square but ran on towards the temple, using a controlled lope to steady her breathing. Snow dusted the paving but the clouds had parted and a brilliant vista of stars blazed in the sky.

She glanced up at them, glad of a final glimpse of the Goddess in her fiery form, and it occurred to her that in dumping her body in the spring, the Fada would unwittingly accommodate her wish to end her days in the Goddess's watery embrace.

She entered the pillars keeping her gaze on the door ahead. The pillars were shrouded in darkness, but she had no fear of attack; her punishment lay within. Lamplight spilled from the doorway and she braced herself and stepped inside. The temple seemed deserted and she went forward, her eyes on the spring.

Its dark waters were ringed by lamps set on ornate stone pedestals and their light showed that flagstones, large and rough-hewn, ran right to the water's edge. The stone denied the roots and shoots of things that grew their rightful place at the Goddess's side and its angles forced the Goddess into an unnatural shape.

Perhaps it was Her contortion that leant the space its oppressiveness *or* the stone ceiling that crouched above, obliterating the stars. Shards of jagged stone protruded down from it, like bigger versions of those Etaine had seen in caverns, but these had been hewn with metal.

The malevolent presence of Fada was all around her but as she moved steadily forward her attention was caught by something suspended above the spring. It turned slowly, sometimes in lamplight and sometimes in shadow, and as she drew closer, she saw it was the true-Eadar child with the beribboned stick; the child the age Ellair would have been had he lived.

He was naked; strung up by the ankles; his bloodied eye-sockets emptied of sight, and as he slowly rotated, she saw his arms had been bound to clasp a stone god to his chest in an obscene parody of worship.

The slate-eyed Fada stepped from the shadows in front and Etaine sensed movement behind and felt the cut of a spear tip on her back. Other Fada moved forward too but Etaine kept her shocked eyes on the child and the slate-eyed Fada smiled and glanced that way too.

It was only for an instant, but an instant was all she needed. She flung her first knife at him, sensed it was not a clean hit but immediately dropped into a crouch and threw herself backwards knocking the legs from under the Fada behind her and ruining his comrades' aims.

Angry shouts erupted and she slashed sideways, was showered with blood and as a spear clattered to the stone, seized it and swept the lamps from their stands. Flaming oil ran across the floor and as Fada leapt clear, Etaine rolled back up onto her feet and smashed down more lamps. The dark was small defence but she stared into light while they strained into darkness.

She had time for two more knives to find their marks as Fada rushed her again and then astonishingly, shouts turned to confusion as other blades flashed and there were thuds as Fada fell. Etaine threw herself sideways as a spear skimmed her shoulder then a blow to the side of the head sent her spinning and she crashed to the floor.

The impact smashed the air from her lungs and as she lay spread-eagled, she had the strange sensation the floor had dissolved and she had sunk to somewhere deeper. The darkness thrummed with anger and she wondered if she were dead but then the Light Way roared back filled with the grunts of battle and the stench of blood and oil.

Rangers fought Fada in the darkness, she realised in astonishment, but Caitlin's whereabouts hammered her, and she staggered in the direction she sensed the slate-eyed Fada had gone. His blood trail led to a stone wall and, as she half fell against it, the wall pivoted to reveal a passageway.

Her shadow shambled along before her but the passage was not long and terminated in a barred door that had been flung wide. It was a holding cell for Fada victims, realised Etaine, as she drew her sleeve-knives. The slate-eyed Fada was bent over Caitlin but whether he strangled or stabbed her, Etaine did not know. She simply plunged her knives into his back, pulled them out, and plunged them in again.

In out, in out; killing the Fada who had killed the child she loved; who had robbed her of joy and happiness. In, out, in out; the gore was up to her elbows, her knives grating on the stone beneath his smashed rib-cage, and then someone hauled her away.

They took the knives from her hands and held her, and Cormac's voice echoed in the distance, beyond her harsh sobs, too far away to reach. And then she was flooded with emerald light and a warmth that returned vision to her eyes and hearing to her ears. Cormac's scent filled her senses and with it came awareness that it was he who held her, and his mouth on hers that, like a honeyed-bridge, had brought her back.

She gazed at him in shock. 'How is it you are here?'

'Did you think I would abandon you, Etaine? Never again; never, *ever* again.'

Asgall appeared in her line of vision and then Beathan supporting Caitlin, who managed a shaky smile. 'We need to be quit of this place, Toiseach,' said Asgall.

Cormac nodded, shifted his grip to Etaine's hand and

hauled her back along the passageway into the temple. There were no signs of Fada bodies or weapons, and the child's body had gone too. Arturo and Bress bucketed water from the spring to wash the floor clean of blood and oil and Asgall helped sweep the broken lamps into the furthest corners.

'There is one more,' said Cormac urgently, glancing at the lightening sky beyond the window.

Arturo and Bress hurried off and Beathan set Caitlin down and collected a bucket of water to clean Caitlin's cell. Then the final Fada was weighted and slipped into the water.

'Not much left of him,' said Arturo, as the body disappeared.

'You have done well,' said Cormac quickly. 'Where are the rest?'

'In the spring,' said Bress. 'I begged the Goddess's forgiveness but Arturo says the darker ways were already unquiet.'

'I felt it in my cell,' said Caitlin hoarsely, her throat already bruising. 'Almost worse than the stinking Fada. There is a terrible anger somewhere deeper in the stone.'

'We need to get back,' said Cormac. 'Arturo, Asgall and Beathan, take the western route. Walk as if you have had a late night and too much mead. Bress and I will bring Caitlin and Etaine.' He was already pulling off his jacket. 'We will be lovers who have been first to brave the icy chill to seek the Goddess's blessing on Bride's Day, and being courteous, we will not have our fair companions suffer the cold.'

Cormac slipped his jacket over her bloodied one and buttoned it up, and Bress helped Caitlin into his, pulling the collar up to hide her swollen throat. Then they strolled back through the pillars and out into the gloom.

It had snowed again and the only footprints belonged

to Arturo, Asgall and Beathan. It meant no Fada lurked nearby, but they did not delay. Fada would soon arrive to relieve their comrades and not find them, but it would not stop the killing. While the snow might keep the Eadar abed a little longer, in the end, they would enter the temple and not come out.

27

Bress walked in front with his arm around Caitlin but
Etaine was barely aware of them, overwhelmed with
the sense of Cormac's nearness, not just the warmth of
his embrace, or the touch of his chest at her shoulder, but
the wonder of him. *Did you think I would abandon you,
Etaine? Never again; never, ever again.* She had gone into
the temple expecting to find death and had found Cormac all over again, and on Bride's Day too. Yet she was
not naïve about the threats that remained; Cormac's other hand rested on his knife and she mentally checked her
boot-knives were still in place.

Cormac did not speak but the Emerald Way held them
both and there was no need for speech there. He loved and
wanted her but coupling on Bride's Day risked another Ellair and dread remained like a wall between them. Arturo
had told Bress the earth was unquiet and even Caitlin had
sensed it and she was not true-Eadar: *There is a terrible
anger somewhere deeper in the stone.* In the Serpent Way?

The streets remained deserted and they reached the
tavern without incident and made their way up the laneway to the yard at its back. Etaine was glad to see Asgall,
Arturo, and Beathan safely there but the yard was also

crowded with Rangers who had quit their beds. Bress had Caitlin enclosed in a hug that showed no signs of ending, and the relief of the waiting Rangers was obvious.

'Bress told me,' said Cormac softly. 'It is why I included him in the attack. I did not think I had much chance of coming back and only took Asgall and Beathan because they threatened to return their signes if I did not, and that was *before* I told them the truth about Boath.'

He ran the backs of his fingers down her cheek, careless of those who saw. 'I feared I would not be in time,' he said, his voice suddenly ragged. 'You did well to fight so many *and* to save Caitlin. Fada do not understand love for they have none in them, but it has to stop, Etaine. The Eadar cannot afford to lose you; *I* cannot afford to lose you.'

Etaine became aware that Bress hovered nearby. 'Yes,' said Cormac, not taking his eyes from her.

'Caitlin heard much of what Fada plan for Bride's Day, Toiseach. They were careless in her hearing as you would be in front of an Eadar you plan to murder, but they taunted her too.' Etaine felt Cormac's attention shift and she turned as well. 'While the Fada enjoy killing us, their aim is to replace the Serpent with their own gods. They have prepared Adam's folk by claiming Bride's Day is special to their gods too, and by building their temples over the springs.'

'To reassure the Maor their precious trade will continue despite the Goddess's absence,' commented Cormac acidly.

Bress nodded. 'They boasted to Caitlin that while the Eadar refuse to reveal the Serpent's lair, in death they will draw it to the surface and so betray the very demon they profess to love.'

'So murdered Eadar are to be used as bait,' said Cormac slowly.

Bress nodded again.

'I felt the Serpent's anger in the temple,' said Etaine. 'But what it might do is Unremembered.'

'But even if they *could* bring the Serpent to the Light Way, they have no weapons that could injure it,' said Cormac.

'The temple ceiling,' said Etaine suddenly. 'Did you see it? It was covered in huge spear-points of stone.'

'You think they mean to drop the ceiling on the Serpent?'

'It is the only explanation. The stone was not decorative.'

'That is not the worst of it,' continued Bress grimly. 'According to Caitlin, Fada believe the Eadar and the Serpent are inextricably linked. Kill the Serpent and the Eadar will dwindle and die too.'

There was shocked silence as those present digested the appalling possibility and Etaine reluctantly turned her eyes to Cormac's. He was silent too but the question as to whether she would risk another child hung in the air between them. Seeding a child provided entry into the Serpent Way but Etaine wondered whether the Serpent actually *allowed* the seeding, and if the Serpent were destroyed, whether any true-Eadar child would be born again.

'We . . .' she began, but that moment there was the sound of running feet and the band sprang into defensive positions. They heard the challenge of Cormac's guards and after a brief pause, the footsteps sounded again and four Rangers emerged from the gloom. Aileg and Fearghas from Dermot's band, and Morgan and Tad from Niall's. Etaine sensed Cormac's tension escalate, along with her own and that of the other Rangers. Both Ceannards sending urgent messages to Cormac *at the same time* could only bode ill.

The Rangers had run hard and it was a moment before they could speak and then their news was eerily similar.

Strange happenings had been reported at Duath and Deas Nathairs deep in the night. Those celebrating Bride's Day Eve nearby had sworn the ground vibrated, a claim dismissed as them having imbibed too much mead *until* tavern-keepers near the squares reported mugs had rattled on their shelves.

Then cracks were noticed in the squares' paving that Adam's folk and Eadar alike insisted had not been there before. The cracks had disappeared under a layer of snow and concerns had eased, but then ructions had sent great waves of water from the springs that washed the snow away, and late night visitors claimed the cracks had grown bigger. The springs seemed calm and concern had eased once more until rumours emerged of grating sounds from under the temples.

'And Fada?' asked Cormac.

'They blame these *dangerous happenings* on the Eadar's *demonic gods* and on Eadar, of course,' said Fearghas. 'Fada have flocked to their temples to aid *their* gods drive the Serpent back into the darkness, which at least has cleared the streets of their foul presence. I am surprised you cannot hear their poisonous chants from here.'

'What of the Maor?'

'They are even more concerned than Fada. When we left, neither Adam's folk nor Eadar would go *anywhere* near Duath and Deas Nathairs *or* the surrounding streets where most the traders are.'

'We do not have much time,' broke in Etaine urgently. 'We have to go back.'

Cormac's expression flashed from incredulity to anger. '*We* are not going back to Iar Nathair and *you* are certainly not going back on your own, even if I have to beg a Maor cell to hold you in!'

'I am not talking about Iar Nathair,' she said impatiently. 'Fada have angered the Serpent and what we are seeing is a small part of what might come. All of Lisanisk could be destroyed and those in it. We have to go back into the Serpent Way.'

Those who heard her words sucked in their breath and their shock infected those who had not.

'Are you sure of this?' asked Cormac. It was a question the Rangers would have expected given the news, but only Etaine and Cormac understood the full significance of the question.

'Yes,' she said, although she had never been less sure of anything in her life. 'We will use your quarters; they are easier to defend,' she said, and strode off. 'And pull the Rangers back beyond the squares,' she tossed over her shoulder. 'The danger will be greatest anywhere near the springs.'

She heard Cormac's quick staccato of orders as she entered his rooms and somehow managed to keep her expression calm as Bress followed her in and rebuilt the fire.

Then Caitlin arrived with her pack and embraced her, careful to avoid her back. 'Thank you for coming for me,' she rasped.

'Rest,' said Etaine softly, and Caitlin nodded and went out.

The fire took the chill off the room and Etaine peeled off Cormac's jacket and then her own jacket and shirt, stiff with Fada blood. Her arms were crusted with it too and she poured water into the bowl and began to wash.

She tried to see their coupling as nothing more than a strategy to defeat Fada, but her stomach churned. They would only be able to enter the Serpent Way if they seeded another child and everything favoured them doing so: it was Bride's Day when the Goddess smiled most strongly on such unions; she and Cormac had seeded a child before; and their link in the Emerald Way was close to complete. But doubt gnawed that something vital was missing and she sensed it was trust.

Despite Cormac having followed her to Iar Nathair and his pledge to never again abandon her, she feared he would, and her lack of trust might just be enough to block what they must do to appease the Serpent.

The door opened behind her, but she did not turn, just heard Cormac come in and slide the bar back into place. He did not approach her either but the thunderous ructions in the Emerald Way told her he stared at her scarred back. She turned, and although his eyes blazed emerald at the sight of her breasts, he made no move towards her.

'Not so eager now, Toiseach?' she said dryly. 'Is it my disfigurement that douses your passions or my faith-lessness?'

'It was *I* who abandoned *you*, Etaine, and you did what you must to survive. And as for your scars, they remind me how I failed you, for nothing could dim your brightness. Your beauty shines like the stars in this Way and in the Emerald one where we already walk together.'

Still his reluctance was plain and she wondered whether, despite his denial, it stemmed from anger over Lagan. 'But?'

'This is not how I yearned for it to be in all the long years since you left.'

'And how did you yearn for it to be?'

Cormac half shrugged but his face was full of pain. 'That you would turn your shining emerald eyes to me as you did seven years ago; that you would take my hand as you did then as your chosen mate; that you would lead me under the oaks and love me again—willingly for my own sake, not for the sake of the Eadar.'

Something woke in Etaine, like the flare of a lamp that dissipates the dark and she went to him and cradled his face between her hands. It was a harder face than seven years ago, more lined and honed, as was her own. The

Goddess's stars were not in her eyes this time but in her heart and at last she understood they burned truly.

'I chose you seven years ago, Cormac, and I have doubted that choice many times since, but not now, not *this* Bride's Day. So it is that I choose you again, Cormac, as my mate; freely and willingly, as is a she-Eadar's right. I want *you* and I want the chance of another child. I want back what Fada sought to rob me of; I want hope and I want love.' She managed to smile. 'But we cannot have the oaks.'

'The beams are oak,' he said thickly, then reached into his pocket and pulled out a silver triskele on a fine chain and slipped it over her head. 'I traded for this in Inschbain seven years ago. My heart knew then what my head did not but I have carried it since in the hope this day would come again.'

Etaine touched the shining spirals that signified the two, the one and the three of the Goddess. 'Come,' she said. 'We have waited long enough.'

Cormac was like a stranger to her and yet more familiar than herself. The sensual swirl of his maleness; the muscles that ridged beneath his skin; his scent and tenderness and need that fed her passions, stirring and sating them in turn. His caresses fired her blood, his kisses filled her with sweetness, and his hardness as he entered her, was at once the soft star-burst of firedrakes and their brilliance, bright in the night sky.

She held him enclosed and he surrendered so that together they rode the bond of their unbroken bodies into the emerald light. And in the moment of two made one, they knew the third; part of each and yet part of neither. Then they were in the Emerald Way, clothed, their clasped hands a lesser reflection of their joining in the Light Way.

'It is not as it should be,' said Etaine as she stared about. The light throbbed and the air thrummed as if a spear parted it. Cormac reached for his knife and cursed to find himself unarmed. 'Weapons have no place here,' said Etaine. 'What soothes or stirs the Emerald Way is different from the Light Way.'

'It is definitely stirred,' said Cormac tersely, his keen gaze searching the mists. 'You have been here often. How do we enter the Serpent Way?'

'I thought you being here with me and the other . . .' She stopped, overcome with wonder at what sparked into being inside her and then wonder was drowned by fear. 'Do not leave me!' she cried.

'How could I leave you, beloved, when we are one?' His mouth found hers and she clung to him, drawing his love and strength to feed what grew, until her heart ceased its hammer and she could breathe again. The sound of a stream came to her and she searched for it amongst the shifts of emerald light.

'The Goddess,' she murmured, and led Cormac forward. Tumbles of stone emerged from the veils and the shadow-forms of trees, only to be swallowed again and still the tinkle of water drew them. Then something moved in the mist and Cormac's hand flashed to his absent knife again and he ground his teeth.

'A she-Fuaran,' whispered Etaine, and bowed. Cormac bowed too and the Fuaran beckoned. They followed her deeper into the mist and more stone appeared, and then a cavernous entranceway so dark Etaine hesitated.

Cormac lengthened his stride so his body was between her and whatever lay within, but the darkness was so intense only the Fuaran's silvery aura allowed them to follow her. They went on deeper into the tunnel and the sense of disquiet grew until it pressed upon them like a living creature.

Cormac's hand tightened on Etaine's and then the darkness gave way to a larger, lighter cavern and they gazed about in astonishment. Lamps of emerald glass sent sinuous emerald shadows sliding around the walls and there were many Fuaran crowded around a raised stone platform. The formality of the gathering reminded Etaine of her hand-fasting to Lagan but there was no joy here; just a sense of urgency. The cavern was heavy with threat and dull rumblings deep in the stone made the emerald shadows ripple and writhe.

'I do not like the feel of this,' whispered Cormac.

'Neither do the Fuaran,' said Etaine. 'They are glad we are here.'

'We should leave.'

'The Fuaran are not our enemies,' said Etaine.

'Nor our friends!'

'They saved me after Craith, Cormac. They carried me from the Hall's ruins down into the Goddess's water, deep underground and I have seen them since near Her springs and streams. They are older than us and wiser but I sense it is *us* they need now.'

The she-Fuaran gestured to the platform and Etaine moved forward taking Cormac with her and then the Fuaran turned them so they faced each other and placed Etaine's hands in Cormac's.

Other Fuaran wreathed them in vines of emerald flowers and as the flowers' perfume filled the air, the mote within Etaine shone like a gem.

'We are joined in the Light Way,' she said softly, as Remembering returned, 'and now we are joined in the Emerald Way.'

The Fuaran began to sing, deep woody notes that swelled and pulsed in endless waves around the walls, chasing the emerald shadows until they blended and were one.

And as the emerald music flowed through Etaine and Cormac and the third they had created, the halves of their link touched to form an arc as bright as molten metal, exquisite in its symmetry.

And then it was gone *and* the cavern, and the music nothing more than an echo eaten by the dank smell of stone.

28

They were in a tunnel that curved away in front and behind and while the Fuaran's cavern had carried a sense of unease, it was so potent here it oozed down the walls like water.

'The Serpent is agitated,' said Etaine. 'It is why the Fuaran were afraid.'

'We need to find a way out,' said Cormac.

He took her hand and they set off but they had not gone far before Etaine realised the tunnel's curve tightened. 'I think we are walking inside a spiral,' she said, and her heart quickened as she recalled the carvings in Cairn Toul's cleft and the circuitous approach to Lisanisk's springs, and she touched the silver triskele at her throat in wonder.

'If it *is* a spiral then we are walking towards its centre,' said Cormac. 'We need to turn back.'

'The Serpent Way is not the Light Way, Cormac. The Goddess means us to follow the spiral to Her heart.'

'Are you sure? We do not have time for mistakes. It must be close to dawn in the Light Way and lovers already visiting the temples.'

'The Serpent Way is *not* the Light Way,' she repeated

and then the floor shook and grit rained from the ceiling. Cormac sheltered her with his body and the mote roused and sucked at her strength. She clung to him and felt the golden flow of his love and protection feed her and their child but it was some time before she could stand unaided.

'At last I truly understand why you took Lagan,' he gasped, 'and how desperate you must have been.' The tunnel rumbled again and Cormac braced himself against the wall to keep them both upright.

'We are running out of time,' cried Etaine. 'We *have* to reach the spiral's centre.' She caught his hand and they went on as quickly as the heaving floor allowed. The tunnel roof sent storms of stinging grit and the sound of the stone's grating was horrendous, and then the tunnel opened into a broad cavern filled by a large brown pool and floating on its surface, or lying pale and shadowy just below, were the mutilated corpses of Eadar.

Etaine buried her face in Cormac's jacket and desperate to summon something beautiful to counter the horror, gripped the triskele at her throat. Memories of the Light Way flooded back: brilliant dawns in the crags; a stag's russet pelt, warm against the snow; an owl's yellow eyes, lit by the moon. The glories of the Emerald Way followed more easily and she raised her head and opened herself to what the Serpent Way offered.

Anger was all about her, slow-grown but no longer quiet, like fire-coals whipped to flame by squalling winds. And even as she recognised it, she felt it escalate. 'Hold me,' she whispered urgently to Cormac, 'and do not move.'

She turned her back to him and as his arms tightened around her, slid her arms over his and held them close. His chest pressed against her scars but she pushed back hard against him so that no space divided them.

In the Light Way their bodies joined, he-Eadar with she-Eadar; in the Emerald Way their hands clasped, as if in a hand-fasting ceremony, and here, in the Serpent Way, their arms twined as adders do in coupling.

A blast of chill air engulfed them as if the roof had fallen in and torn a hole into the snowy dawn of the Light Way, and then the water from the pool stormed upwards, taking with it the bodies of the slain Eadar. It was like watching a mighty waterfall in the crags except one that roared skywards not fell to earth.

Even if Etaine had wanted to follow where the water and its obscene cargo went, the whip of wind and water prevented it. She felt Cormac's body shudder as he fought to hold them both against its mighty suck and then just as abruptly as it had begun, the column of water was gone. Etaine drew a careful breath but kept her grip on Cormac's arms so that he remained as still as she.

And then the blast of icy air repeated, but this time the roaring column of water *was* a waterfall; it issued from above and again carried bodies with it. They were Fada, realised Etaine in shock, and with them were the smashed pieces of their temples and broken effigies of their gods. The wreckage crashed into the pool but instead of generating a mighty wave to engulf the cavern *and* Etaine and Cormac, it pierced the pool's surface with scarcely a ripple and kept on going. And then it was gone too and the cavern quiet again.

The pool was tranquil too but something moved in its depths. For a moment Etaine thought a Fada body drifted back to the surface but then realised it was a reflection. Light glinted off flecks of sinuous movement and, dry-mouthed with fear, she raised her eyes to the walls. They were no longer of stone but of muscle and skin; of over-lapping scales that bunched and stretched as the Serpent tightened its coils about them.

Cormac's breathing was as harsh as her own and she knew that, like her, he feared the Serpent would wreak revenge on *them* for the spring-fouling blood of the in-nocents; for the temples that crouched where stars should have shone; for the Eadar's long neglect.

The coils drew ever closer and still neither of them moved. Etaine kept her grip on Cormac but the link between them was so strong that he shared what she Remembered. The Serpent's mighty head uncoiled and swung towards them and Etaine forced herself to meet its gaze.

The Serpent's scales shone like burnished metal but its golden eyes held depths that Etaine sensed were older than the times of Eadar and Fuaran and shifters; of the wild's creatures; perhaps even of the land itself. And then, imperceptibly, the Serpent lowered its head and Etaine felt the mote inside her blaze. Cormac jolted but Etaine's fear vanished as she understood the Serpent's satisfaction with what it found.

The two, the one and the three; the Light and Emerald and Serpent Ways; the Goddess uncoupled, coupled and crone; the Serpent and the Goddess one, but also the three, and it was the eyes of the third, the crone, that she glimpsed in the endlessness of the Serpent's golden gaze.

And then it was gone, or *they* were, and it was Cormac's dark emerald eyes she stared into as he surrendered himself to her and to what they had created. She released him then and pulled him into her arms, cradling his head to her breast until his breathing quieted and he was at peace, and then they slept.

29

Etaine roused first and struggled to make sense of what had happened. The fire had burned low which gave her a feel for how much time had elapsed, as did the silvery light that edged the shutters. The blankets were deliciously warm and she was entwined with Cormac as she had been in the Serpent Way but with the physical intimacy of the Light Way. His scent clothed her skin and she lowered her head and kissed along the curve of his jaw and then his lips.

Cormac's dark emerald eyes opened and he pulled himself onto his elbow. His gaze was full of love but she sensed the Toiseach in him reassert itself and what they shared in the Emerald and Serpent Ways begin to slip away.

'We are one, Etaine,' he reassured her.

'And Eadar Rangers,' she replied, steadying. 'Time to see what evil Fada have wrought in our absence.'

He kissed her deeply and then more lightly, swung himself off the bed and dressed. She dressed too, staring down in wonder at her belly as she buttoned her shirt, then pulled on her underwear and trousers and methodically strapped on her belt-knives. Those she had left embedded in Fada at Iar Nathair had been cleaned and returned to her pack and she buckled on her sleeve-sheaths, slid the knives in, and pulled down her cuffs.

Cormac watched her as she secured her boot-knives and she saw how troubled he was. 'You should rest today,' he said.

'I have no need of rest. Besides, I can only rest if you rest with me,' she reminded him.

'I do not want you to fight.'

'I am a Ranger.'

'But no longer of my band.'

Etaine grimaced. Cormac was right; she had been outcast since she had hurled her signe at his feet but she resented being reminded of it. Her hand closed over the triskele at her throat and memories of the Serpent hummed. Its power was terrible but easier to deal with than the complications that beset her now.

'As I am outcast, I will fight alone,' she said, and headed for the door.

Cormac caught her arm. 'The Maor allowed us entry to Lisanisk on condition the Rangers remained under my command.'

'That is not my problem, Toiseach,' she snapped.

She felt his turmoil escalate in the Emerald Way and stopped. It was natural for him to fear the loss of his truemate, she realised, and it was a fear she shared. If Cormac were killed she would have to make the agonising decision to take another mate or follow him into death and take their child with her.

'I should not have forced—' he began, but she placed her fingers on his lips.

'I *chose*, as is a she-Eadar's right and I do not regret my choice. But I sense this is not about you or me, or our child, or even the Eadar. It is about the Ways in the times Unremembered. The Fuaran serve the Serpent but they need the Eadar to enter the Serpent's realm where they cannot tread. I think the shifters are part of it too; that they understand the Serpent's demand for new life. We felt the Serpent's anger and saw the destruction it wrought but I do not Remember enough to know whether what we witnessed happened in the Serpent Way or in the Light Way or both.'

'You Remember more than I do,' he said tersely.

'And through me, you will Remember too,' she said, and gently ran her fingers through the heavy silk of his hair. Braid-beads caught the last of the firelight and as his mouth came to hers, the mote within her glowed and grew. Their kiss was long and sweet and when it ended she rested her forehead against his. 'The two, the one, and the three,' she murmured. 'The Goddess has blessed us, Toiseach.'

'Yes, but now it is time to return to the Light Way.' She nodded and together they stepped out into the yard.

The air was chill and the snow that covered the paving churned to a slush by many feet. Rangers milled about in the confined space and were clearly relieved to see them. News of what Etaine and Cormac were to attempt had spread and while the Serpent Way was Unremembered, the perils of the Serpent were imprinted on every Eadar brain.

Cormac summoned Asgall and Beathan and they moved off, deep in conversation and then Caitlin appeared at Etaine's side. Her neck was mottled with bruising but she was back to her usual cheerful self.

'It has been a busy night all round,' she rasped. 'Messengers have sprinted back and forth between the bands and while Asgall and Beathan have not shared their news, rumours are a lot thicker than this snow.' She kicked at the slush and then chaffed her hands. 'Come into the tavern, Etaine. It will be warm there and you need to eat.'

The tavern was crowded, which was surprising given the earliness of the hour, but those gathered looked more fearful than festive. Their voices were muted but their exchanges still easy to over-hear and they centred on the astonishing fact that Fada and their temples had been swallowed by the springs.

Etaine struggled to reconcile the night's events with the morning's news but the arrival of bowls of steaming soup and fresh oaten-bread helped her calm enough to focus on what she heard as she ate.

Some of Adam's folk and lesser-Eadar recounted explosions of water from the springs while others said that at Iar Nathair, the Serpent had actually raised its head and glowered about. But there were stories that were whispered, of how the surging waters had brought with them the mutilated bodies of Eadar.

The Guard had been called but Fada had swarmed from their lodgings to block the Guard's access to the squares. Fada had denied all knowledge of Eadar corpses, which had disappeared again in any case, and had persuaded the Guard their stone gods would restore order in time for trading to begin.

Fada had disappeared into their temples and their chants had kept those in the nearby taverns wakeful until, sometime after midnight, there had been a terrible crack. Adam's folk had rushed from their beds to find gaping holes where the temples had stood and no sign of Fada.

The Guard now prevented access to the squares but Lisanisk's inhabitants were in no hurry to go anywhere near the surrounding streets, let alone the shattered remnants of what had enclosed the springs. There were Adam's folk who insisted the crack had been lightning bolts, despite the skies being snowy rather than stormy, but the improbability of bolts striking three temples at once was obvious to Adam's folk and lesser-Eadar alike.

'Of course, you and Cormac know what really happened,' said Caitlin softly. 'I Remember enough to know that one way or another, you were there in the Serpent Way when you coupled last night. Even the Rangers who have yet to Remember speak of it.'

'I had not realised it was such a public event,' said Etaine uncomfortably.

Caitlin laughed. 'Oh, it was alright, but you did not have to be guarding you to know you had joined; it resonated in the Emerald Way so strongly I sensed it in my sleep.'

Etaine felt the joy of their coupling surge through her afresh but all too soon, doubt and fear followed. Caitlin touched her arm. 'Your coupling was a moment of beauty and a long one at that,' she added with a grin, 'but now you wonder, as I did, whether the risk was worth it and whether it would have been better to fight on alone.'

'I am still not sure of him,' muttered Etaine, aware as she said it that Cormac sensed her doubt.

'It takes a little while for both parties here in the Light Way,' acknowledged Caitlin, 'but I have Remembered there is no such doubt in the Emerald or Serpent Ways.'

The conversations around them faltered but Etaine knew of Cormac's approach long before he led his Rangers into the tavern. Adam's folk watched them warily, as if they wondered for the first time at the Eadar's link to the Serpent. The young red-haired server showed no such reservations as he cheerily delivered bowl after bowl of soup and platters of bread, and the tavern's conversations slowly picked up, as if Adam's folk were reassured by Eadar needing to eat like normal folk.

Cormac sat beside her but continued his speech with Asgall and Beathan who also joined their table. Etaine was content now he was near and the child was quiet within her. She rested her hand lightly on her belly and felt again the Serpent's satisfied gaze and yet it came to her once more that the Serpent did not have to contend with the

Light Way's difficulties.

The reality was that Etaine's true-mate was a Toiseach who had sworn to lead the Rangers until next Bride's Day; that Fada spears could await them beyond the shattered squares; that Maor might believe it was Eadar who threatened their lucrative trade and not Fada. And if the Maor *did* believe that?

'Etaine?'

Cormac's dark emerald eyes were on her as were the eyes of the rest of the table and she realised he had probably had to call her more than once to get her attention.

'She-Eadar are entitled to be a little vague at certain times,' said Caitlin innocently, 'and on certain occasions to eat more than usual,' she added, as she started on a second bowl of soup.

'The Ceannards' reports accord with the stories circulating here,' said Cormac. 'I have called in the bands and as soon as they arrive, we will march down to Iar Nathair. It is the main spring and where Adam's folk and lesser-Eadar are gathering. Any surviving Fada are likely to go there too. We have heard nothing from the Maor or Guard but I am guessing they will be there *and* the traders. I am hoping for a discussion but we must be prepared for a fight.'

Etaine's muscles bunched as she considered the distance to the gate; the Gate Guard; and the open lands between Lisanisk and the forests.

'Fada might have persuaded Maor the Serpent acted under our orders,' continued Cormac, 'and we know from Craith that Adam's folk might side with them, especially if they are frightened. Even so, I do not think they will join in any attack. They are more likely to expel us.'

'Expelling us won't solve their problem with the Serpent,' pointed out Etaine. 'We need to persuade them that only we can soothe it.'

'That might be difficult. Fada have had years to seed

suspicion of us and now there is fear here as well.'

'Just like Craith,' muttered Etaine. 'At least Fada no longer have their temples to hide their murderous activities in.'

'They will continue to murder nevertheless, although given the numbers that rushed to their temples to repel the Serpent, I am not sure how many have survived.'

'And what we witnessed last night might have happened in many places, not just here,' said Etaine.

The confusion at the table was obvious but understanding dawned on Cormac's face, helped by her link to him in the Emerald Way. Time was different in the Emerald Way, as Caitlin had once pointed out to her, and nor could the Emerald Way be traversed like the Light Way, by crossing crags and fording rivers. And the Serpent Way was different again.

She and Cormac had witnessed Eadar and Fada corpses and the smashed remains of temples, and had assumed they came from Lisanisk, but they might have come from Fada temples anywhere and *anytime*.

Her heart leapt at the possibility Fada had been scoured from the lands and she knew Cormac felt her hope surge in the Emerald Way but before he could speak, Dermot appeared at their table and Cormac's attention swung to him. Their brief exchange told her the other bands waited outside and she rose with the rest of the Rangers and followed Cormac out.

30

Cormac kept them in tight defence formation as he led them through Lisanisk's streets and despite Etaine being outcast, he ordered her into the middle ranks between Asgall and Beathan. They had witnessed her altercation with Cormac when she had hurled her signe at his feet but were also aware of what had followed. But there might another reason why Cormac had chosen his closest friends as her protectors: Arturo had disappeared.

It was possible he had fallen victim to a Fada spear but Etaine sensed nothing amiss in the Emerald Way and a certainty settled over her that, having fulfilled his pledge to the Fuaran, he had returned to the wilds. Arturo had been a greater part of her life over the years than Cormac and his departure now, without proper farewell, left her disorientated.

What unfolded had confirmed her suspicions that Fuaran directed shifters to ensure the Serpent was served, but what if too many years of Unremembering had passed, and the Serpent been offered only Eadar death and not the new life it demanded? Then the violence at the springs might be but a taste of what was to come.

And despite the Fuaran and shifters' long struggle,

she, Cormac, and their unborn child might still be slaughtered before the day was out.

No one challenged them in their march through the predawn light but the Rangers went with their hands on their weapons. The narrow streets and double-storeyed houses favoured Fada spear-throwers and the streets' quietness was unsettling, as were the traders' stalls, bereft of custom. The traders hovered beside their wares and Etaine was relieved to see their faces become hopeful rather than hostile at the sight of the Rangers.

Cormac nodded to them courteously but did not stop and as the square came into view the reason for the deserted streets became clear. Etaine's hands flashed to her knives and the Rangers drew swords and set arrows. It seemed all of Lisanisk was gathered there and when the Rangers came into view, they turned as one and fell silent.

There was no sign of Fada grey amongst the crowd and Etaine's head swivelled as she calculated the distance to the nearest houses. They were well within spear-range and her attention swung to the far side of the square where the street ran away towards the gate. Every instinct screamed at her to flee but Cormac led them inexorably on.

The crowd parted to let them through and closed behind them and while those gathered kept a respectful distance, the square reeked of a trap.

Cormac had never been caught by Fada; branded; and watched his child die. Panic threatened but his reassurance in the Emerald Way was swift, as was access to his plans, and she calmed as she realised his strategy had the potential to be more powerful than any show of weapons strength.

His dark emerald eyes, white skin, and black hair a flash with Eadar-crafted beads displayed the full potency of a true-he-Eadar and the Rangers he led held the greatest concentration of true-Eadar blood Lisanisk had ever seen.

In marching his full retinue of Eadar Rangers into their midst, Cormac reminded them these lands had belonged to Eadar *and* to the Serpent long before their ships had found its shores. Etaine sensed a shift in the Rangers too. Eadar were not given to arrogance or swagger but their bearing reflected the rightness of their place in the Light and Emerald and Serpent Ways.

Adam's folk felt nothing of the Emerald Way but lesser-Eadar sensed the glory of the days Unremembered and many were hand-fasted to Adam's folk, so even *if* Adam's folk were in thrall to Fada, Etaine sensed the ties to their lesser-Eadar mates would stay their weapon-hands.

Cormac called a halt on the very edge of the square and still no one spoke. Adam's folk watched warily and the Rangers' weapons remained at the ready, and then the crowd stirred as several silver-haired Maor made their way forward. Maor had joined in Craith's slaughter and as the group neared Cormac, a ferocious protective instinct woke in Etaine and she stepped sideways to clear her aim.

It was Beathan who again restrained her, but with none of his former anger. 'Wait,' he whispered. His love for Cormac was no less than her own and Etaine clenched her jaw and waited. Cormac's orders rang out for them to lower their weapons and the band complied as Etaine did, but she kept her knives unsheathed.

Cormac was in discussion with the Maor who looked to be the most senior, and while she was too distant to hear their speech, the shift of emotions in the Emerald Way was clear. The Maor was anxious about the delay to Bride's Day festivities, *to trading*, but there was a fear there too that permeated the entire crowd. They rightly feared whatever had destroyed the temples but they also feared the Eadar, as if they had suddenly realised that Eadar were part of something powerful and perilous *and unseen*.

Craith had proved how easy it was to turn fear into a

murderous want to destroy and Etaine braced herself for the shout of Fada voices; for accusations and recriminations and demands for the Eadar's annihilation, but the gentle morning remained quiet. It gave Cormac the opportunity he needed and Etaine was already moving up through the ranks before his summons of her sounded in the Light Way.

She came to his side and if the Maor had not noticed the power of mate-paired true-Eadar before, they did now, as did those gathered. But another power clothed Etaine and Cormac, subtler but no less potent: that of the third and Etaine laid her hand lightly on her belly to reinforce the point.

In the Emerald Way, her proximity gave Cormac the words she Remembered more perfectly than he, and his voice rang out across the gathering. 'Lisanisk has long been a place of importance,' he began. 'Here the Fuaran thanked the Goddess *and* served the Serpent, and while you have built a mighty trading settlement that honours the paths the Fuaran trod, *and* you honoured the Goddess each Bride's Day, the Serpent has been neglected.'

Silence stretched and it was the senior Maor who broke it. 'What should be done?' he asked.

'The Serpent needs little to remain content. It needs no gold or silverware; no finely woven cloth or shining coin. The Serpent is of life and demands only that life be honoured. The oaks that drew their life-giving sap from the Goddess's waters have been cut down, and the creatures lost that lived in their holes and hollows; that grazed between their boles; that nested in their branches. The rich earth that edged the Goddess's water has been crushed by a stone that denies the roots of reed and sedge; that breaks the Goddess's true form.'

Cormac's voice hardened. 'Instead of life, the Serpent has been offered death: in *your* settlements and beyond *your* walls, and on *this* day, the Goddess's *special* day, here at the springs. The Serpent is angry, but you have seen but a small part of its anger; only a small part of the destruction the Serpent can wreak, for in *this* day's darkness, I and my true-mate have soothed the Serpent in the hope that you will see no more.'

The senior Maor conferred with the other Maor and it was not long before he turned back to the Rangers. 'We will ensure the Serpent is served as you have described,' he said, 'and the springs are returned to how they once were. But we must know whether the danger of *this* Bride's Day has passed.'

Etaine knew the danger would never pass; that it extended far beyond the lives of those gathered here in the Light Way but what Cormac had achieved was no small thing. He had defeated the Fada without having named them, let alone raised swords against them in battle.

'We will ensure the Serpent is at rest, so the happy celebrations of Bride's Day can proceed as they should,' he said.

The Maor were so relieved they actually bowed and most of the crowd followed suit. Etaine waited while Cormac called the Ceannards to him and addressed them quietly and then he returned to her side and together they walked out onto the square. Snow lay over the stone, a soft lilac blanket unmarked by prints, and Etaine kept the pace slow to imbue their steps with solemnity.

'And *is* the Serpent at rest?' murmured Cormac, as they neared the spring.

'As much as it will ever be. And with so many Fada dead, I feel almost placid myself.'

'They will rebuild.'

'I do not sense they can. The Maor have had a taste of the damage the Serpent can inflict on their precious trade *and* on their settlements and they won't risk a repeat. The best Fada can hope for is to trade like everyone else but they have never been interested in trade. I think the few who remain will seek other shores for their vile gods.'

'It would be useful to summon the Serpent at need,' said Cormac.

'No one *summons* the Serpent, Cormac,' said Etaine dryly.

They reached the edge of the smashed paving and stopped. 'What now?' he asked.

Etaine stared up at the pale sky, yet to be touched by the new day's gold, and then down at the broken paving. It was a stark reminder of Fada brutality and she longed to be far from the places that bore their loathsome marks.

'It would be fitting to circle the Goddess's blessed waters three times,' she said slowly, 'once for each of Her forms. If nothing else, it will reassure Adam's folk the danger has passed.'

'So be it, true-mate,' he said, and they set off, hand in hand. As they walked, Etaine thought of the child they had seeded seven years before, of the one she now carried, and of the path she had turned down. She still had no idea where it led.

They completed the first circuit and came back to their starting point. 'Once for you and me and Ellair, the child I never knew,' said Cormac softly, as they set off once more.

They completed their second circuit and his hand tightened on hers. 'Once for you and me and the child I *will* know, and love as I love you,' he said.

They set off for the final time and came to a stop where their prints showed they had begun. 'Once for you and me and our child, and for what the future will bring,' he said gravely.

They bowed to the Goddess and then Cormac turned and took Etaine's hands in his. Those gathered still watched from the edge of the square, but he held her as if they were alone.

'When this day is done, if you are willing, we will go east to your kin or to mine. We will make our home there and raise our child in peace as the Serpent requires. The Rangers will choose another Toiseach, although like you, I sense the need for one is now small.'

Etaine's throat tightened, holding her silent but she knew that in the Emerald Way, Cormac felt her love for him burn bright and their child grow strong.

She drew him to her and they kissed. It was a long kiss as befits Bride's Day and at that moment the sun breached the world's soft curve and the spring's still waters shone. A cheer erupted from the waiting crowd and they streamed onto the square.

'A fair Bride's Day to you, true-mate,' said Etaine solemnly.

'And to you,' returned Cormac, and then hand in hand, they walked back to their comrades over the glittering snow.

End of The Emerald Serpent

Check out the book trailer:
https://www.youtube.com/watch?v=bGpKxnpCEMg

I hope you enjoyed *The Emerald Serpent*. **Authors need reviews!** It's how our readers find us. I would love you to leave me an honest review on Amazon, Goodreads or another of your favourite reader sites. Enjoy **free** short stories? Visit my website, sign up for my newsletter, and read *The Gift* and *The Tale of Prince Anura*.

Works by KS Nikakis

Available on Amazon KDP and a range of digital platforms

Non Fiction

Journey: Seeking the Sacred, Spirit and Soul in the Australian Wilderness – *For fans of Joseph Campbell's hero journey*

When we set out into the wilderness, what is it we *really* seek?

Do we seek new sights or do we seek new selves? And are we really on one journey or on two?

Journeying fifteen thousand kilometres into Australia's blood-red heart, Nikakis discovers that every journey is perilous, for travellers risk carrying the clutter of their outer lives with them; a clutter that blinds them to the other journey they crave; that of the inner *soul-journey* into a deeper understanding of self.

To enter Australia's vast Outback wilderness, is to enter a place of endless horizons; a place doused with brilliant gold dawns and dazzling sunsets; a place silvered by star-encrusted night skies and, most importantly, a place of hidden sacred places in whose deep stillness our inner journeys can at last unfold.

In the spirit of travellers like Robert Macfarlane and Scott Stillman, Nikakis asks what it is we really see, feel and understand when we follow in the steps of those who have gone before us deep into the wilderness.

Drawing on her Ph.D. in Joseph Campbell's hero myth, and using original poetry and novel extracts, Nikakis takes us on this second journey; a journey of the sacred, spirit and soul, where our inner selves finally have the time and space to gift us richer and more fully-realised lives.

Fantasy Novel Series

Angel Caste 5 Book Series – available complete in one book or as five individual books:

Angel Blood, Angel Breath, Angel Bone, Angel Bound, Angel Blessed.

Angel Caste – Complete 5 Book Series – *A modern female hero on a timeless quest*

A troubled half-angel, a beautiful angel guide, a binding promise . . .

Viv is on day release from jail to attend the funeral of the thug she thinks is her father, when she comes face to face with her real father, the powerful angel Archae Kald. If finding out she's a half-angel isn't shocking enough, Viv discovers her mother isn't dead after all but lost somewhere in the tangle of worlds called the Rynth.

Determined to find the only person who has ever truly loved her, Viv transits to Kald's angel world where he appoints the beautiful Thris as her guide. Thris is kind and caring, unlike the males Viv has known before, but after living on the streets, Viv finds it impossible to trust.

Friendship grows as Thris trains her to travel the rifts, but the Rynth is a dark and dangerous place, even for angels and, as Thris grows increasingly tempted by Viv's emerging angel traits, disaster strikes.

Viv journeys on alone and stumbles into a war zone where she finds a lost child, who she pledges to take to safety but, as the war rages on, deciding who is friend and who is enemy becomes a deadly game of chance.

Bound by his promise to guide Viv to her mother, Thris embarks on a desperate search for her, but a greater threat confronts them both and, in the end, they must fight not just for their own lives, but for the lives of those they love.

The Kira Chronicles 6 Book Series - available complete in one book or as six individual books:

The Whisper of Leaves, The Silence of Stone, The Secrets of Stars, The Thunder of Hoofs, The Crying of Birds, The Music of Home.

The Kira Chronicles – Complete 6 Book Series – *traditional fantasy with deep forests and high stakes*

A gold-eyed Healer, a prophecy, two brothers at war.

In seasons long past, twin gold-eyed princes sundered a

kingdom. Rejecting his brother Terak's warrior ways, Kasheron led his people deep into the great southern forests and established the healing settlement of Allogrenia. The Tremen flourished, upholding Kasheron's legacy of peace and healing, and protected by the vast, trackless trees.

All Tremen delight in the healing arts, but Kira is the greatest Healer of them all.

To the north of Allogrenia, drought ravages the Shargh's land and, as their suffering escalates, the chief's younger brother seizes on an ancient prophecy to snatch the chiefship for himself. The prophecy links the Shargh's doom to a gold-eyed Healer, and Kira has gold eyes.

The Shargh attack with devastating consequences and Kira must fight to save the wounded, but the Shargh wounds rot, no matter her skill, and Kira finds herself in a deadly race against time. As the slaughter continues, she makes the horrifying discovery that the Shargh hunt *her*. To halt the attacks and save her people, she sets off for the North to seek aid from her long-sundered warrior kin.

But the dangers beyond the forests exceed even the Shargh attacks. The Tremen detest their warrior kin but Terak's descendants have inflicted a worse fate on the Tremen. Kira's new-found love is torn apart by ancient hostilities and when trust turns to betrayal, it risks everything she has fought for.

As the battles rage on, Kira becomes increasingly sickened by the bloodshed and, desperate to end the suffering once and for all, she sets out on a quest that could cost her everything and everyone she loves.

Fantasy Novels

Heart Hunter – *A female hunter on an impossible quest*

Fleet is a young Sceadu hunter: skilled, strong, and fast. She hunts deep into the ice-bound mountains in a desperate search for meat, for the rains have failed and plunged her people into hunger. Her hunts are long and dangerous but she has much to look forward to. Soon the Sceadu's shaman will gift Fleet her air-name and then she will be free to marry Ashin, the man she loves.

But while Fleet is on hunt, the old shaman dies, and the new shaman dreams a very different future for her. Fleet must cross the frozen, impenetrable mountains and return water and fish to the Sceadu's streams—or lose Ashin forever. And there is a second *secret* quest, even deadlier than the first, that if Fleet fails, threatens the Sceadu's very existence.

Fleet refuses the quest for the shaman wants Ashin too, but in a moment of anger and frustration, she breaks the hunter's most sacred law and sets out into the snow-swept mountains to pay with her life.

It is the start of a perilous journey that takes Fleet deep into the earth's darkest places, into hostile new worlds, and even into Death itself. She discovers that nothing is as it seems and that to survive, she must draw on every shred of her hunter strength. Doing the impossible, it turns out, is just the beginning.

The Third Moon – *Science fantasy with a very human quest*

Where does the past end and the future begin?

Warrain is haunted by inherited memories of his people's dispossession and the theft of their children, and when he is just twelve years old, the nightmare repeats. But Warrain isn't living on Earth in the 21st Century but on the planet Imago in the far flung future.

Five years before, Station One's Mech's got high on the opioid arrash and, in the bloodshed that followed, Warrain's scientific community were expelled from the Station, his father murdered, and his mother and unborn sibling lost to him.

The scientists carve out a rudimentary Station high in Imago's ranges and Warrain's friends get on with their lives but not Warrain. He climbs the Tors to stare down at Station One, dream of his mother and sibling, and plot revenge.

And then one day, everything changes. A third moon appears in the sky, one of Imago's life-forms calls him by name, and disease breaks out at Station One.

When Mechs visit to seek help for their ill, Warrain seizes the opportunity to deal them a blow they will never forget. But the third moon brings changes that threaten them all and, to aid the life-form whose kind is being dispossessed and slaughtered, he must turn his back on the hate that has long sustained him and find another way to live.

Messenger – *a dystopic future filled with hope*

In a world made deaf by hatred, who will hear the messenger?

Severine's world ends the day her Traveller family is murdered. Being raised in their loving gay community marked her as an outsider, but being female doubled the danger. Women are scarce, precious, and hunted.

When chance brings Severine face to face with the father she has never known, he assigns, Jeph, the son of his murdered friend, as her guard. They soon clash and Jeph is glad to deliver her to the Enclaves, the sanctuary her father carved out for his community's women and children.

But there is no safety in a world broken by war and sickness and when violence follows her, Severine sets out for the northern city of Andhaka, in search of a home among her mother's people. Pledged to protect her, Jeph follows, but the north holds nothing for him except terrible danger.

It's been years since Andhaka welcomed outsiders with anything but bullets, and to survive and protect Jeph, Severine must learn to use her enemies' weapons against them.

As the stakes rise, she comes to understand what drove her father north seventeen years before and his quest becomes her quest. But she hasn't counted on the savage legacy war and sickness have left behind, or on falling in love.

I Heard the Wolf Call My Name – *gender-fluid shifters in search of home*

Finalist Best YA Novel – 2019 Aurealis Awards

Jax is just twelve years old and in bird-form high above his island home, when it explodes, killing everyone on it. Believing himself to be the only survivor, he is shocked to come face to face with his boyhood friend, Matiu, ten years later.

Matiu is military and the military needs shifters for a crucial mission, but Jax refuses. Having spent ten long years burying his bizarre shifter past, he isn't about to resurrect it. But Matiu rouses other feelings too that Jax finds harder to ignore.

As the military ramps up pressure to force Jax's cooperation, he shifts to bird-form and flees to the last remaining island, where he crashes in the middle of Anahera's vision-quest.

She searches for her skin-spirit animal to transform her into Ikaika, a protector of her people. She dreams of finding the white-wolf but finds Jax instead and to save him, she must abandon her quest.

Her kindness only adds to Jax's turmoil. To decide who he truly is and where he really belongs, he must first confront his painful past but that isn't the worst of his problems. The forces that blew Jax's island out of existence threaten Anahera's as well, and he might be the only shifter who can save it. But time is running out.

Fantasy Short Stories

The Gift – A Deep Fantasy Short Story #1 – free on my website at www.ksnikakis.com

Excerpt:

Thariel sat for a long time, surveying all around her, as if she ate the world that would soon be memory. Then she took the harness from the mare, and with soft words, thanked her and bade her farewell. Her own feet she turned towards the forest, tossing her face-plate aside as she went, so that her hair fell loose to her waist, then she discarded her chest-armour, the sword and dagger, her bow and quiver.

The trees closed in and she came at last to the lake Men call Menios and stood for a while on its shore. An owl cried and a mouse shrieked, and all around her the souls of the newly dead jostled in their journey to the void.

She stepped into the water and the new life inside her quivered. 'Fear not, little one,' she whispered, in her own tongue. 'We are going home.'

The Tale of Prince Anura – A Deep Fantasy Short Story #2 – free on my website at www.ksnikakis.com

Excerpt:

I should have been happy, for she was beautiful. Dark rivers of curls, skin as white as moonlight on water, breasts softer than spawn, and she loved me well. But her chamber was small, no matter the comfort of her bed, and the old feelings of entrapment rose, as persistent as gas that bubbles from rot below still waters.

I sat at the casement and listened, as I had once loitered near the watery skin of the second world and waited. The moon grew large and small many times, but it came at last, as I knew it would.

The soft lament on the night-time air, the song of a soul as confined as mine. It took me a journey of many days through the depths of a massive forest to find her tower.

Stone it was and sheer, and as remote as the third world's glimmer had once been. I sang to her and she answered with sweet melodies of her own and we made love as frogs do, with our voices. And when trust had built, she let down her shining ladder of golden hair.

Glass-Heart – A Deep Fantasy Short Story #3
Finalist Best YA Short Story – 2019 Aurealis Awards

Excerpt:

Geth moved amongst his band, exchanging quiet words while they waited. Some he had fought with since the Tallon's foul ships had first found their shores while others had come later, when the burn of cot and kin had sent them from their valleys.

Hate drove them but hate was no shield against arrow and knife. It was fighting skills that kept them hale, and Geth ensured they had them aplenty. He needed them living, not just for their own sakes and his, but for what would come later. When the Tallon's stain had been scoured away, the destroyed must be rebuilt.

Kyth sat alone and he went to her and gazed about. 'The glass-heart's fled, has it?'

'I sent her to a place of safety. She will come to me when it is over.'

'Safety was what I wanted for you!'

'And what I wanted for Nyar.' Her eyes caught the star-sheen as she looked up at him. 'But you cannot always have what you want, can you, Ceannasai?'

Dragon Sprite – A Deep Fantasy Short Story #4

Excerpt:

Genn rocketed straight upwards, not just because she enjoyed seeing the limitless blue sky before her, but because a Waiwin's wing shape made vertical flight harder for them. Orin didn't try to catch her but swept in circles around her, gaining height in an ever-narrowing spiral. It was a clever tactic and one Genn didn't believe he had thought of in the instant she had cleared the trees. He had obviously studied her strategies and developed a plan to counter them *or so he thought*.

Genn waited until the spiral narrowed to *axeel*, the minimum distance a Waiwin must keep from a Velven unless she *accepted* him, then swerved towards him, narrowing the distance between them. Orin's eyes flashed to black, shocked she *had* accepted him, but before he could act, she folded her wings and dropped.

The strength that had driven Orin's pursuit had surged to his wing-tendrils in anticipation of locking them with hers and he would struggle even to stay airborne until it flowed back.